THE GLASS MENAGERIE

TENNESSEE WILLIAMS

THE GLASS MENAGERIE

HIGH SCHOOL EDITION

WITH A TEACHING GUIDE BY KATE WALKER

A NEW DIRECTIONS BOOK

Library of Congress Cataloging-in-Publication Data
Names: Williams, Tennessee, 1911–1983, author. | Walker, Kate, writer of high school guide | Bray, William Robert, 1951– writer of introduction.
Title: The glass menagerie : high school guide / Tennessee Williams ; introduction by Robert Bray.
Description: New York : New Directions Books, [2019] | Audience: Grade 9 to 12. | "A New Directions book."
Identifiers: LCCN 2018049336 | ISBN 9780811227308 (alk. paper)
Subjects: LCSH: Young men—Drama. | Young women with disabilities—Drama. | Mothers and sons—Drama. | Mothers and daughters—Drama. | Brothers and sisters—Drama. | Families—Drama. | Saint Louis (Mo.)—Drama. | Williams, Tennessee, 1911–1983—Study and teaching (Secondary)
Classification: LCC PS3545.I5365 G5 2019 | DDC 812/.54—dc23
LC record available at https://lccn.loc.gov/2018049336

New Directions Books are published for James Laughlin
by New Directions Publishing Corporation
80 Eighth Avenue, New York 10011

CONTENTS

INTRODUCTION

Notes on *The Glass Menagerie*

On December 26, 1944, as much of the nation dialed their radios to the pivotal Battle of the Bulge raging in Belgium, a nervous young playwright fretted over matters closer to home. As he paced about waiting for the curtain to rise at Chicago's Civic Theatre, his apprehension was not unwarranted. Last minute rehearsals had not gone well, backstage feuds had been threatening on-stage chemistry, and icy weather had almost shut down the city. There was also his bitter memory of a previous disaster almost exactly four years earlier, when an uninitiated Tennessee Williams had endured humiliation and profound discouragement at the calamitous Boston opening of *Battle of Angels,* the first of his plays to receive a major production. Traveling around the country in virtual penury for a couple of years after this disaster, Williams eventually landed an initially promising but briefly-held Metro-Goldwyn-Mayer contract in Hollywood. Here he toiled haplessly as a hired scriptwriter while he worked on his own plays (including what would become *Menagerie*) and complained about a "sort of spiritual death-ray that is projected about the halls of Hollywood."

Although he had been sketching *Menagerie* since the late 1930s, his full concentration on this still-evolving play while at MGM was probably the result of thoughts turning toward home. Just prior to Williams's arrival on the West Coast in 1943, his sister Rose had undergone a prefrontal lobotomy in St. Louis, and it might well be argued that on one level *The Glass Menagerie* represents Williams's attempt to come to terms with his sister's illness and perhaps exorcise his guilt over not having taken more measures in trying to prevent the operation. At MGM, while writing what he called "celluloid brassieres" for actresses such as Lana Turner, Williams also kept drafting *Menagerie* and eventually offered a screen version of the play (then called *The Gentleman Caller*) to MGM (who would later lose a bid-

1

ding war for its screen rights). Tennessee Williams's ultimate goal, of course, was to reach Broadway, but Williams and company made the decision to open in Chicago "before we brave the New York critics." Working through problems leading up to opening night, the playwright still faced many last minute obstacles, including admonitions by producer Eddie Dowling and others to make significant changes in the script. But by virtue of Williams's resilience, the play's superior material, the fine acting, and perhaps sheer good fortune, his dogged pursuit of fame was suddenly being realized. As the reviews came in and the show prepared to move to New York's Playhouse Theatre (where it would run for 563 performances), there was the sense that a remarkable transformation was taking place in American theatre. Although audiences were profoundly moved by the pathos of the Wingfield household and the almost mythical performance of Laurette Taylor as Amanda, it was this *new playwright,* with his southern manner, poetic language, and dramaturgic legerdemain, who most fascinated critics and theatre aficionados. Now the sudden object of adulation, Tennessee Williams became an immediate, if bemused, celebrity. Still trying to come to terms with his new status some three years later, he described this turning point as his being "snatched out of virtual oblivion and thrust into sudden prominence" by "the catastrophe of Success."

As Williams worked on various play scripts during the period just prior to his completing *The Glass Menagerie,* he was simultaneously occupied with formulating a new aesthetic of theatre. An habitué of the movies since his childhood, Williams was now experimenting with a more fluid dramatic structure that would to some extent emulate the cinematic technique of *mise-en-scène,* the method by which a film director stages an event for the camera. Arguing for the necessity of a "sculptural drama," Williams wrote, "I visualize it as a reduced mobility on the stage, the forming of statuesque attitudes or tableaux, something resembling a restrained type of dance, with motions honed down to only the essential or significant." (An immediate example of this technique comes to mind in the final scene of *Menagerie,* where, Madonna-like, Amanda is seen consoling Laura.) Williams's stage "innovations" were somewhat recycled from European expressionism, but when the elements of his "plastic theatre" (with its emphasis more on the *representation* of reality) were combined with his exquisite romantic lyricism, the result represented a formidable new force on the American stage.

Today one can easily understand why American audiences of the 1940s, weary of realism and prosaic dialogue, eagerly embraced Williams's protean gifts in this rather static and predictable theatre climate. The timing was propitious for his novel voice. Yet why does this play *continue* to hold our fascination; to engage the talent of such actresses as Helen Hayes, Jessica Tandy, Katharine Hepburn, and Joanne Woodward; to inspire translations into languages from Arabic to Tamil; to engender four movie adaptations; to enjoy productions ranging from high schools to London's Haymarket; and to be scrutinized by almost countless literary analyses? More than fifty years after the Wingfields first took to the stage, this dysfunctional family is as popular as ever.

It is no mere coincidence that many of our most memorable American plays, from *Long Day's Journey into Night*, through *Death of a Salesman* and *Who's Afraid of Virginia Woolf* up to *Buried Child*, depict familial tensions and alienations, the give-and-take of domestic warfare. Indeed, the venerable tradition of dramatizing family strife is by no means uniquely American, as this motif transcends cultures and predates Shakespeare's *Hamlet*, even going back to the drama of Aeschylus. Tennessee Williams certainly realized that positioning crises of the heart within the immediate family would provide ample material for audience empathy and catharsis, as virtually anyone can identify with similar levels of emotional conflict.

Williams's family years spent in St. Louis were some of the unhappiest of his life, and when asked by an interviewer what first brought him to New Orleans, Tennessee said, "St. Louis." For Williams, writing *Menagerie* was an experience born of grief, "the saddest play I have ever written. It is full of pain. It's painful for me to see it." His composing this play forced him toward compelling reminiscences of his own family life, particularly the misunderstandings between him and his mother and the sadness of Rose's existence.

The parallels between the Williams/Wingfield families have been well established by Williams and his biographers. In St. Louis the Williamses inhabited a rather modest apartment after having suffered a wrenching move from their pastoral, socially prominent existence with the Dakins (Williams's maternal grandparents) in Mississippi. Like the play's inconsolable narrator, Tennessee (then known as Tom) worked at a shoe company while dreaming of becoming a writer. Williams's sister Rose (the model for Laura) was extremely troubled; and most people who knew her well admitted that Edwina Williams was "the spitting image" of Amanda. Tom did bring home a gentleman caller for Rose, and his sister actually had a glass menagerie, although their brother Dakin remembers it as "just two or three pieces ... very cheap little things, probably purchased at Woolworth's." Although it could be said that most of Williams's writing is to some extent autobiographical, it is important to remember that for the obvious parallels, there are also significant deviations. First, during the St. Louis years depicted in the play, the younger brother also occupied the Williams apartment, and Williams's father, Mr. Cornelius Williams (unlike Mr. Wingfield), was usually present after working hours. As Dakin Williams recalls, "My father was home all the time, and that was one of the major problems of our family." In searching for autobiographical connections to Williams's plays, then, one should come to regard Williams's *oeuvre* not as a duplication of actual experience but as an organic holograph, synthesized and embellished from experience, analogous to Monet's series of cathedral studies or Gauguin's depictions of island life. From these painful St. Louis years Williams extracted enough material to write a story that is completely accessible yet deceptively complex.

As the fractured world of the Wingfields unfolds, the first apparent fissure is the societal anonymity into which they have fallen, for they live in "one of those vast hive-like conglomerations ... as one interfused mass of automatism." Collectively marginalized, as individuals in search of identity they fare even worse. Amanda, Laura, and Tom live out secret horrors, all the while unsuccessfully trying to conceal or repress their respective demons from each other. As a result, *Menagerie* reveals the story of family members whose lives form a triangle of quiet desperation, each struggling with an individual version of hell, while simultaneously seeking escape from the gravity of each other's pathologies.

In fact, patterns of escape form a leitmotif that help structure the play, as every character seeks flight; if not literally, then through the imagination. Mr. Wingfield, the "telephone man who fell in love with long distances," becomes the first fugitive from the "hive-like conglomeration." His prominently looming, smiling photograph and "Hello—Goodbye!" postcard suggest that he suffers no regret over his departure. Victimized himself by this abandonment, Tom's own inevitable choice between sacrifice and personal freedom thus becomes all the more difficult. Yet Tom's vicarious adventures "at the movies" must eventually give way to his fire-escape exit for the Merchant Marines, and he departs "attempting to find in motion what was lost in space." But his departure exacts a severe price, as he finally realizes that Amanda's and Laura's confinement will force them even further into their respective worlds of jonquils and glass unicorns. Although Tom eventually follows his father's footsteps, the inextinguishable candles of his sister, like the Ancient Mariner's albatross, will forever curse his journey. Tom may perform his own version of "Malvolio the Magician" and vanish from the Wingfield apartment/coffin, but he must eventually return to retell his story, using other magical tricks (such as framing the action and then "disappearing" back into it) to validate his point of view. Furthermore, Tom's various complexities—he is the prototypical Williams artist/dreamer/romantic/misunderstood outsider—identify him as one of Williams's most easily recognizable "fugitive kind," demonstrating just how thinly art can veil biography.

Tom might be a daydreamer, but Amanda's grasp of reality is the most tenuous of all. She ameliorates her pathetic existence with fabricated memories of gentleman callers and the faded promise of what could have been. Her poetic raptures, particularly during her memorable "jonquils" tableau, transport her back to a time and place when life consisted of promising choices. These ramblings, which function almost as interior monologues, seem to be a fuzzy, out-of-focus juxtaposition of the perhaps with the improbable (were there really *seventeen* gentleman callers?) and underscore the degree to which Amanda can escape back in time, far away from the exigencies of the St. Louis apartment to another dimension where light bills get paid, where the verandah appropriates the fire escape, where the scheduling of her beaux becomes her most pressing concern. Ironically, her idealized past becomes her unrealized wish for her daughter's future happiness—but this hope contrasts pitiably with the actual prospects for Laura's finding a mate. Usually in denial about Laura's likelihood of happiness, Amanda is forced to face the truth after the Gentleman Caller fiasco, thus lashing out at Tom and verbally acknowledging for the first time that she is a "mother deserted" and that her "selfish" son has an "unmarried sister who's crippled and has no job." Audiences and readers may choose either to demonize Amanda or regard her as a misguided saint, but the complexity of her character (suggested initially by Williams's description in the *dramatis personae*) precludes any facile assessment of her motherhood. By wanting the best for her adult children but attempting to dictate the terms by which they live, Amanda is a mother to whom all must remain ambivalent.

Whereas fabricating an idealized past becomes Amanda's compensation for her present existence, Laura's retreat into the world of her glass animals provides her only imaginative escape. With her almost pathological shyness and complete vulnerability, Laura becomes symbolically positioned alongside the animals on her shelf. Unable to hold a job or even complete a typing course, her reclusive withdrawal from the outside "world of lightning" would seem to insulate her from further chaos—until the promise of a relationship emerges.

Into the Wingfield's triangle of despair comes the excruciatingly banal, "nice, ordinary young man" named Jim O'Connor. Jim is one of those characters, who, like Mitch in *A Streetcar Named Desire,* aspires to normalcy and is entirely successful. Even somewhat more one-dimensional than other Williams cut-outs, Jim believes in the "Zzzzzp!" of democracy and in the System's "Century of Progress." Moreover, he maintains complete confidence in the future— paradoxically, a sure sign that he holds no membership in Williams's "visionary company." When Jim's arrival threatens Laura's insulation from the outside world, her first impulse is flight, the fitting reaction of a wounded creature. As the visit progresses, so does her ephemeral dalliance with the world of normality. In one of the most brilliant and symbolically charged moments of the play, the breaking of the unicorn's horn, we are briefly led to believe that Laura's curse has been lifted, especially after the kiss. However, the brief romantic interlude is followed by the jarring, horrific news of Betty, and at that point, the shattering of the unicorn assumes a darker meaning. Although Jim's "courtship" of Laura is not mean-spirited, neither is it thoughtful; and when "He grins and ducks jauntily out," Jim departs relatively oblivious to the damage he has left behind, the world of broken unicorns and Laura's shattered dream of companionship.

With this "memory play" Tennessee Williams transports us into private worlds where desire clashes with obdurate reality, where loss supplants hope. After more than half a century we continue to be drawn to a play that explores so many aspects of the human condition. With this first great artistic success of his new "plastic theatre," Williams demonstrated how he could synthesize music, poetry, and visual effects into compelling emotional situations, structurally underpinning them with symbolic moments so arresting that theatregoers depart the aisles—and readers turn the last page—enriched with an assortment of moments guaranteed to haunt the receptive mind. Williams once described *Menagerie* as "my first quiet play, and perhaps my last." From this quietness, however, his characters' cries of desperation will continue to reach out for understanding as long as we are there to listen.

Robert Bray

THE GLASS MENAGERIE

nobody, not even the rain, has such small hands

E. E. Cummings

THE CHARACTERS

AMANDA WINGFIELD *(the mother)*
A little woman of great but confused vitality clinging frantically to another time and place. Her characterization must be carefully created, not copied from type. She is not paranoiac, but her life is paranoia. There is much to admire in Amanda, and as much to love and pity as there is to laugh at. Certainly she has endurance and a kind of heroism, and though her foolishness makes her unwittingly cruel at times, there is tenderness in her slight person.

LAURA WINGFIELD *(her daughter)*
Amanda, having failed to establish contact with reality, continues to live vitally in her illusions, but Laura's situation is even graver. A childhood illness has left her crippled, one leg slightly shorter than the other, and held in a brace. This defect need not be more than suggested on the stage. Stemming from this, Laura's separation increases till she is like a piece of her own glass collection, too exquisitely fragile to move from the shelf.

TOM WINGFIELD *(her son)*
And the narrator of the play. A poet with a job in a warehouse. His nature is not remorseless, but to escape from a trap he has to act without pity.

JIM O'CONNOR *(the gentleman caller)*
A nice, ordinary, young man.

CAST LISTING AND SCENE

The Glass Menagerie was first produced by Eddie Dowling and Louis J. Singer at the Civic Theatre, Chicago, Illinois, on December 26, 1944, and at the Playhouse Theatre, New York City, on March 31, 1945. The setting was designed and lighted by Jo Mielziner; original music was composed by Paul Bowles; the play was staged by Eddie Dowling and Margo Jones. The cast was as follows:

THE MOTHER	Laurette Taylor
HER SON	Eddie Dowling
HER DAUGHTER	Julie Haydon
THE GENTLEMAN CALLER	Anthony Ross

SCENE: *An alley in St. Louis*

TIME: *Now and the Past*

Part I. Preparation for a Gentleman Caller.

Part II. The Gentleman calls.

AUTHOR'S PRODUCTION NOTES

Being a "memory play," *The Glass Menagerie* can be presented with unusual freedom of convention. Because of its considerably delicate or tenuous material, atmospheric touches and subtleties of direction play a particularly important part. Expressionism and all other unconventional techniques in drama have only one valid aim, and that is a closer approach to truth. When a play employs unconventional techniques, it is not, or certainly shouldn't be, trying to escape its responsibility of dealing with reality, or interpreting experience, but is actually or should be attempting to find a closer approach, a more penetrating and vivid expression of things as they are. The straight realistic play with its genuine Frigidaire and authentic ice-cubes, its characters who speak exactly as its audience speaks, corresponds to the academic landscape and has the same virtue of a photographic likeness. Everyone should know nowadays the unimportance of the photographic in art: that truth, life, or reality is an organic thing which the poetic imagination can represent or suggest, in essence, only through transformation, through changing into other forms than those which were merely present in appearance.

These remarks are not meant as a preface only to this particular play. They have to do with a conception of a new, plastic theatre which must take the place of the exhausted theatre of realistic conventions if the theatre is to resume vitality as a part of our culture.

THE SCREEN DEVICE: There is *only one important difference between the original and the acting version of the play* and that is the *omission* in the latter of the device that I tentatively included in my *original* script. This device was the use of a screen on which were projected magic-lantern slides bearing images or titles. I do not regret the omission of this device from the original Broadway production. The extraordinary power of Miss Taylor's performance made it suitable to have the utmost simplicity in the physical production. But I think it may be interesting to some readers to see how this device was conceived. So I am putting it into the published manuscript. These images and legends, projected from behind, were cast on a section of wall between the front-room and dining-room areas, which should be indistinguishable from the rest when not in use.

The purpose of this will probably be apparent. It is to give accent to certain values in each scene. Each scene contains a particular point (or several) which is structurally the most important. In an episodic play, such as this, the basic structure or narrative line may be obscured from the audience; the effect may seem fragmentary rather than architectural. This may not be the fault of the play so much as a lack of attention in the audience. The legend or image upon the screen will strengthen the effect of what is merely allusion in the writing and allow the primary point to be made more simply and lightly than if the entire responsibility were on the spoken lines. Aside from this structural value, I think the screen will have a definite emotional appeal, less definable but just as important. An imaginative producer or director may invent many other uses for this device than those indicated in the present script. In fact the possibilities of the device seem much larger to me than the instance of this play can possibly utilize.

THE MUSIC: Another extra-literary accent in this play is provided by the use of music. A single recurring tune, "The Glass Menagerie," is used to give emotional emphasis to suitable passages. This tune is like circus music, not when you are on the grounds or in the immediate vicinity of the parade, but when you are at some distance and very likely thinking of something else. It seems under those circumstances to continue almost interminably and it weaves in and out of your preoccupied consciousness; then it is the lightest, most delicate music in the world and perhaps the saddest. It expresses the surface vivacity of life with the underlying strain of immutable and inexpressible sorrow. When you look at a piece of delicately spun glass you think of two things: how beautiful it is and how easily it can be broken. Both of those ideas should be woven into the recurring tune, which dips in and out of the play as if it were carried on a wind that changes. It serves as a thread of connection and allusion between the narrator with his separate point in time and space and the subject of his story. Between each episode it returns as reference to the emotion, nostalgia, which is the first condition of the play. It is primarily Laura's music and therefore comes out most clearly when the play focuses upon her and the lovely fragility of glass which is her image.

THE LIGHTING: The lighting in the play is not realistic. In keeping with the atmosphere of memory, the stage is dim. Shafts of light are focused on selected areas or actors, sometimes in contradistinction to what is the apparent center. For instance, in the quarrel scene between Tom and Amanda, in which Laura has no active part, the clearest pool of light is on her figure. This is also true of the supper scene, when her silent figure on the sofa should remain the visual center. The light upon Laura should be distinct from the others, having a peculiar pristine clarity such as light used in early religious portraits of female saints or madonnas. A certain correspondence to light in religious paintings, such as El Greco's, where the figures are radiant in atmosphere that is relatively dusky, could be effectively used throughout the play. (It will also permit a more effective use of the screen.) A free, imaginative use of light can be of enormous value in giving a mobile, plastic quality to plays of a more or less static nature.

TENNESSEE WILLIAMS

THE GLASS MENAGERIE

SCENE ONE

The Wingfield apartment is in the rear of the building, one of those vast hive-like conglomerations of cellular living-units that flower as warty growths in overcrowded urban centers of lower middle-class population and are symptomatic of the impulse of this largest and fundamentally enslaved section of American society to avoid fluidity and differentiation and to exist and function as one interfused mass of automatism.

The apartment faces an alley and is entered by a fire escape, a structure whose name is a touch of accidental poetic truth, for all of these huge buildings are always burning with the slow and implacable fires of human desperation. The fire escape is part of what we see—that is, the landing of it and steps descending from it.

The scene is memory and is therefore nonrealistic. Memory takes a lot of poetic license. It omits some details; others are exaggerated, according to the emotional value of the articles it touches, for memory is seated predominantly in the heart. The interior is therefore rather dim and poetic.

At the rise of the curtain, the audience is faced with the dark, grim rear wall of the Wingfield tenement. This building is flanked on both sides by dark, narrow alleys which run into murky canyons of tangled clothes-lines, garbage cans, and the sinister latticework of neighboring fire escapes. It is up and down these side alleys that exterior entrances and exits are made during the play. At the end of Tom's opening commentary, the dark tenement wall slowly becomes transparent and reveals the interior of the ground-floor Wingfield apartment.

Nearest the audience is the living room, which also serves as a sleeping room for Laura, the sofa unfolding to make her bed. Just beyond, separated from the living room by a wide arch or second proscenium with transparent jaded portieres (or second curtain), is the dining room. In an old-fashioned whatnot in the living room are seen scores of transparent glass animals. A blown-up photograph of the father hangs on the wall of the living room, to the left of the archway. It is the face of a very handsome young man in a doughboy's First World War cap. He is gallantly smiling, ineluctably smiling, as if to say "I will be smiling forever."

Also hanging on the wall, near the photograph, are a typewriter keyboard chart and a Gregg shorthand diagram. An upright typewriter on a small table stands beneath the charts.

The audience hears and sees the opening scene in the dining room through both the transparent fourth wall of the building and the transparent gauze portieres of the dining-room arch. It is during this revealing scene that the fourth wall slowly ascends, out of sight. This transparent exterior wall is not brought down again until the very end of the play, during Tom's final speech.

The narrator is an undisguised convention of the play. He takes whatever license with dramatic convention is convenient to his purposes.

Tom enters, dressed as a merchant sailor, and strolls across to the fire escape. There he stops and lights a cigarette. He addresses the audience.

TOM: Yes, I have tricks in my pocket, I have things up my sleeve. But I am the opposite of a stage magician. He gives you illusion that has the appearance of truth. I give you truth in the pleasant disguise of illusion.

To begin with, I turn back time. I reverse it to that quaint period, the thirties, when the huge middle class of America was matriculating in a school for the blind. Their eyes had failed them, or they had failed their eyes, and so they were having their fingers pressed forcibly down on the fiery Braille alphabet of a dissolving economy.

In Spain there was revolution. Here there was only shouting and confusion. In Spain there was Guernica. Here there were disturbances of labor, sometimes pretty violent, in otherwise peaceful cities such as Chicago, Cleveland, Saint Louis . . . This is the social background of the play.

[Music begins to play.]

The play is memory. Being a memory play, it is dimly lighted, it is sentimental, it is not realistic. In memory everything seems to happen to music. That explains the fiddle in the wings.

I am the narrator of the play, and also a character in it. The other characters are my mother, Amanda, my sister, Laura, and a gentleman caller who appears in the final scenes. He is the most realistic character in the play, being an emissary from a world of reality that we were somehow set apart from. But since I have a poet's weakness for symbols, I am using this character also as a symbol; he is the long-delayed but always expected something that we live for.

There is a fifth character in the play who doesn't appear except in this larger-than-life-size photograph over the mantel. This is our father who left us a long time ago. He was a telephone man who fell in love with long distances; he gave up his job with the telephone company and skipped the light fantastic out of town . . .

The last we heard of him was a picture postcard from Mazatlan, on the Pacific coast of Mexico, containing a message of two words: "Hello—Goodbye!" and no address.

I think the rest of the play will explain itself. . . .

[Amanda's voice becomes audible through the portieres. Legend on screen: "Ou sont les neiges." Tom divides the portieres and enters the dining room. Amanda and Laura are seated at a drop-leaf table. Eating is indicated by gestures without food or utensils. Amanda faces the audience. Tom and Laura are seated in profile. The interior has lit up softly and through the scrim we see Amanda and Laura seated at the table.]

AMANDA [*calling*]: Tom?

TOM: Yes, Mother.

AMANDA: We can't say grace until you come to the table!

TOM: Coming, Mother. [*He bows slightly and withdraws, reappearing a few moments later in his place at the table.*]

AMANDA [*to her son*]: Honey, don't *push* with your *fingers*. If you have to push with something, the thing to push with is a crust of bread. And chew—chew! Animals have secretions in their stomachs which enable them to digest food without mastication, but human beings are supposed to chew their food before they swallow it down. Eat food leisurely, son, and really enjoy it. A well-cooked meal has lots of delicate flavors that have to be held in the mouth for appreciation. So chew your food and give your salivary glands a chance to function!

[Tom deliberately lays his imaginary fork down and pushes his chair back from the table.]

TOM: I haven't enjoyed one bite of this dinner because of your constant directions on how to eat it. It's you that make me rush through meals with your hawklike attention to every bite I take. Sickening—spoils my appetite—all this discussion of—animals' secretion—salivary glands—mastication!

AMANDA *[lightly]*: Temperament like a Metropolitan star!

[Tom rises and walks toward the living room.]

You're not excused from the table.

TOM: I'm getting a cigarette.

AMANDA: You smoke too much.

[Laura rises.]

LAURA: I'll bring in the blancmange.

[Tom remains standing with his cigarette by the portieres.]

AMANDA *[rising]*: No, sister, no, sister—you be the lady this time and I'll be the darky.

LAURA: I'm already up.

AMANDA: Resume your seat, little sister—I want you to stay fresh and pretty—for gentlemen callers!

LAURA *[sitting down]*: I'm not expecting any gentlemen callers.

AMANDA *[crossing out to the kitchenette, airily]*: Sometimes they come when they are least expected! Why, I remember one Sunday afternoon in Blue Mountain— *[She enters the kitchenette.]*

TOM: I know what's coming!

LAURA: Yes. But let her tell it.

TOM: Again?

LAURA: She loves to tell it.

[Amanda returns with a bowl of dessert].

AMANDA: One Sunday afternoon in Blue Mountain—your mother received—*seventeen!*—gentlemen callers! Why, sometimes there weren't chairs enough to accommodate them all. We had to send the colored boy over to bring in folding chairs from the parish house.

TOM [*remaining at the portieres*]: How did you entertain those gentlemen callers?

AMANDA: I understood the art of conversation!

TOM: I bet you could talk.

AMANDA: Girls in those days *knew* how to talk, I can tell you.

TOM: Yes?

[*Image on screen: Amanda as a girl on a porch, greeting callers.*]

AMANDA: They knew how to entertain their gentlemen callers. It wasn't enough for a girl to be possessed of a pretty face and a graceful figure—although I wasn't slighted in either respect. She also needed to have a nimble wit and a tongue to meet all occasions.

TOM: What did you talk about?

AMANDA: Things of importance going on in the world! Never anything coarse or common or vulgar.

[*She addresses Tom as though he were seated in the vacant chair at the table though he remains by the portieres. He plays this scene as though reading from a script.*]

My callers were gentlemen—all! Among my callers were some of the most prominent young planters of the Mississippi Delta—planters and sons of planters!

[Tom motions for music and a spot of light on Amanda. Her eyes lift, her face glows, her voice becomes rich and elegiac. Screen legend: "Ou sont les neiges d'antan?"]

There was young Champ Laughlin who later became vice-president of the Delta Planters Bank. Hadley Stevenson who was drowned in Moon Lake and left his widow one hundred and fifty thousand in Government bonds. There were the Cutrere brothers, Wesley and Bates. Bates was one of my bright particular beaux! He got in a quarrel with that wild Wainwright boy. They shot it out on the floor of Moon Lake Casino. Bates was shot through the stomach. Died in the ambulance on his way to Memphis. His widow was also well provided-for, came into eight or ten thousand acres, that's all. She married him on the rebound—never loved her—carried my picture on him the night he died! And there was that boy that every girl in the Delta had set her cap for! That beautiful, brilliant young Fitzhugh boy from Greene County!

TOM: What did he leave his widow?

AMANDA: He never married! Gracious, you talk as though all of my old admirers had turned up their toes to the daisies!

TOM: Isn't this the first you've mentioned that still survives?

AMANDA: That Fitzhugh boy went North and made a fortune—came to be known as the Wolf of Wall Street! He had the Midas touch, whatever he touched turned to gold! And I could have been Mrs. Duncan J. Fitzhugh, mind you! But—I picked your *father!*

LAURA *[rising]*: Mother, let me clear the table.

AMANDA: No, dear, you go in front and study your typewriter chart. Or practice your shorthand a little. Stay fresh and pretty!—It's almost time for our gentlemen callers to start arriving. *[She flounces girlishly toward the kitchenette.]* How many do you suppose we're going to entertain this afternoon?

[Tom throws down the paper and jumps up with a groan.]

LAURA *[alone in the dining room]*: I don't believe we're going to receive any, Mother.

AMANDA [*reappearing, airily*]: What? No one—not one? You must be joking!

[*Laura nervously echoes her laugh. She slips in a fugitive manner through the half-open portieres and draws them gently behind her. A shaft of very clear light is thrown on her face against the faded tapestry of the curtains. Faintly the music of "The Glass Menagerie" is heard as Amanda continues, lightly.*]

Not one gentleman caller? It can't be true! There must be a flood, there must have been a tornado!

LAURA: It isn't a flood, it's not a tornado, Mother. I'm just not popular like you were in Blue Mountain. . . .

[*Tom utters another groan. Laura glances at him with a faint, apologetic smile. Her voice catches a little.*]

Mother's afraid I'm going to be an old maid.

[*The scene dims out with the "Glass Menagerie" music.*]

SCENE TWO

On the dark stage the screen is lighted with the image of blue roses. Gradually Laura's figure becomes apparent and the screen goes out. The music subsides.

Laura is seated in the delicate ivory chair at the small claw-foot table. She wears a dress of soft violet material for a kimono—her hair is tied back from her forehead with a ribbon. She is washing and polishing her collection of glass. Amanda appears on the fire escape steps. At the sound of her ascent, Laura catches her breath, thrusts the bowl of ornaments away, and seats herself stiffly before the diagram of the typewriter keyboard as though it held her spellbound. Something has happened to Amanda. It is written in her face as she climbs to the landing: a look that is grim and hopeless and a little absurd. She has on one of those cheap or imitation velvety-looking cloth coats with imitation fur collar. Her hat is five or six years old, one of those dreadful cloche hats that were worn in the late Twenties, and she is clutching an enormous black patent-leather pocketbook with nickel clasps and initials. This is her full-dress outfit, the one she usually wears to the D.A.R. Before entering she looks through the door. She purses her lips, opens her eyes very wide, rolls them upward and shakes her head. Then she slowly lets herself in the door. Seeing her mother's expression Laura touches her lips with a nervous gesture.

LAURA: Hello, Mother, I was— [*She makes a nervous gesture toward the chart on the wall. Amanda leans against the shut door and stares at Laura with a martyred look.*]

AMANDA: Deception? Deception? [*She slowly removes her hat and gloves, continuing the sweet suffering stare. She lets the hat and gloves fall on the floor—a bit of acting.*]

LAURA [*shakily*]: How was the D.A.R. meeting?

[*Amanda slowly opens her purse and removes a dainty white handkerchief which she shakes out delicately and delicately touches to her lips and nostrils.*]

Didn't you go to the D.A.R. meeting, Mother?

AMANDA [*faintly, almost inaudibly*]: —No.—No. [*Then more forcibly.*] I did not have the strength—to go to the D.A.R. In fact, I did not have the courage! I wanted to find a hole in the ground and hide myself in it forever! [*She crosses slowly to the wall and removes the diagram of the typewriter keyboard. She holds it in front of her for a second, staring at it sweetly and sorrowfully—then bites her lips and tears it in two pieces.*]

LAURA [*faintly*]: Why did you do that, Mother?

[*Amanda repeats the same procedure with the chart of the Gregg Alphabet.*]

Why are you—

AMANDA: Why? Why? How old are you, Laura?

LAURA: Mother, you know my age.

AMANDA: I thought that you were an adult; it seems that I was mistaken. [*She crosses slowly to the sofa and sinks down and stares at Laura.*]

LAURA: Please don't stare at me, Mother.

[*Amanda closes her eyes and lowers her head. There is a ten-second pause.*]

AMANDA: What are we going to do, what is going to become of us, what is the future?

[*There is another pause.*]

LAURA: Has something happened, Mother?

[*Amanda draws a long breath, takes out the handkerchief again, goes through the dabbing process.*]

Mother, has—something happened?

AMANDA: I'll be all right in a minute, I'm just bewildered— [*She hesitates.*] —by life. . . .

LAURA: Mother, I wish that you would tell me what's happened!

AMANDA: As you know, I was supposed to be inducted into my office at the D.A.R. this afternoon.

[Screen image: A swarm of typewriters.]

But I stopped off at Rubicam's Business College to speak to your teachers about your having a cold and ask them what progress they thought you were making down there.

LAURA: Oh. . . .

AMANDA: I went to the typing instructor and introduced myself as your mother. She didn't know who you were. "Wingfield," she said, "We don't have any such student enrolled at the school!" I assured her she did, that you had been going to classes since early in January.

"I wonder," she said, "If you could be talking about that terribly shy little girl who dropped out of school after only a few days' attendance?"

"No," I said, "Laura, my daughter, has been going to school every day for the past six weeks!"

"Excuse me," she said. She took the attendance book out and there was your name, unmistakably printed, and all the dates you were absent until they decided that you had dropped out of school.

I still said, "No, there must have been some mistake! There must have been some mix-up in the records!"

And she said, "No—I remember her perfectly now. Her hands shook so that she couldn't hit the right keys! The first time we gave a speed test, she broke down completely—was sick at the stomach and almost had to be carried into the wash room! After that morning she never showed up any more. We phoned the house but never got any answer"— While I was working at Famous–Barr, I suppose, demonstrating those— [*She indicates a brassiere with her hands.*] Oh! I felt so weak I could barely keep on my feet! I had to sit down while they got me a glass of water! Fifty dollars' tuition, all of our plans—my hopes and ambitions for you—just gone up the spout, just gone up the spout like that.

[Laura draws a long breath and gets awkwardly to her feet. She crosses to the Victrola and winds it up.]

What are you doing?

LAURA: Oh! [*She releases the handle and returns to her seat.*]

AMANDA: Laura, where have you been going when you've gone out pretending that you were going to business college?

LAURA: I've just been going out walking.

AMANDA: That's not true.

LAURA: It is. I just went walking.

AMANDA: Walking? Walking? In winter? Deliberately courting pneumonia in that light coat? Where did you walk to, Laura?

LAURA: All sorts of places—mostly in the park.

AMANDA: Even after you'd started catching that cold?

LAURA: It was the lesser of two evils, Mother.

[*Screen image: Winter scene in a park.*]

I couldn't go back there. I threw up—on the floor!

AMANDA: From half past seven till after five every day you mean to tell me you walked around in the park, because you wanted to make me think that you were still going to Rubicam's Business College?

LAURA: It wasn't as bad as it sounds. I went inside places to get warmed up.

AMANDA: Inside where?

LAURA: I went in the art museum and the bird houses at the Zoo. I visited the penguins every day! Sometimes I did without lunch and went to the movies. Lately I've been spending most of my afternoons in the Jewel Box, that big glass house where they raise the tropical flowers.

AMANDA: You did all this to deceive me, just for deception? [*Laura looks down.*] Why?

LAURA: Mother, when you're disappointed, you get that awful suffering look on your face, like the picture of Jesus' mother in the museum!

AMANDA: Hush!

LAURA: I couldn't face it.

[*There is a pause. A whisper of strings is heard. Legend on screen: "The Crust of Humility."*]

AMANDA [*hopelessly fingering the huge pocketbook*]: So what are we going to do the rest of our lives? Stay home and watch the parades go by? Amuse ourselves with the glass menagerie, darling? Eternally play those worn-out phonograph records your father left as a painful reminder of him? We won't have a business career—we've given that up because it gave us nervous indigestion! [*She laughs wearily.*] What is there left but dependency all our lives? I know so well what becomes of unmarried women who aren't prepared to occupy a position. I've seen such pitiful cases in the South—barely tolerated spinsters living upon the grudging patronage of sister's husband or brother's wife!—stuck away in some little mousetrap of a room—encouraged by one in-law to visit another—little birdlike women without any nest—eating the crust of humility all their life! Is that the future that we've mapped out for ourselves? I swear it's the only alternative I can think of! [*She pauses.*] It isn't a very pleasant alternative, is it? [*She pauses again.*] Of course—some girls *do marry*.

[*Laura twists her hands nervously.*]

Haven't you ever liked some boy?

LAURA: Yes. I liked one once. [*She rises.*] I came across his picture a while ago.

AMANDA [*with some interest*]: He gave you his picture?

LAURA: No, it's in the yearbook.

AMANDA [*disappointed*]: Oh—a high school boy.

[*Screen image: Jim as the high school hero bearing a silver cup.*]

LAURA: Yes. His name was Jim. [*She lifts the heavy annual from the claw-foot table.*] Here he is in *The Pirates of Penzance*.

AMANDA [*absently*]: The what?

LAURA: The operetta the senior class put on. He had a wonderful voice and we sat across the aisle from each other Mondays, Wednesdays and Fridays in the auditorium. Here he is with the silver cup for debating! See his grin?

AMANDA [*absently*]: He must have had a jolly disposition.

LAURA: He used to call me—Blue Roses.

[Screen image: Blue roses.]

AMANDA: Why did he call you such a name as that?

LAURA: When I had that attack of pleurosis—he asked me what was the matter when I came back. I said pleurosis—he thought that I said Blue Roses! So that's what he always called me after that. Whenever he saw me, he'd holler, "Hello, Blue Roses!" I didn't care for the girl that he went out with. Emily Meisenbach. Emily was the best-dressed girl at Soldan. She never struck me, though, as being sincere . . . It says in the Personal Section—they're engaged. That's—six years ago! They must be married by now.

AMANDA: Girls that aren't cut out for business careers usually wind up married to some nice man. [*She gets up with a spark of revival.*] Sister, that's what you'll do!

[Laura utters a startled, doubtful laugh. She reaches quickly for a piece of glass.]

LAURA: But, Mother—

AMANDA: Yes? [*She goes over to the photograph of Mr. Wingfield.*]

LAURA [*in a tone of frightened apology*]: I'm—crippled!

AMANDA: Nonsense! Laura, I've told you never, never to use that word. Why, you're not crippled, you just have a little defect—hardly noticeable, even! When people have some slight disadvantage like that, they cultivate other things to make up for it—develop charm—and vivacity—and—*charm!* That's all you have to do! [*She turns again to the photograph.*] One thing your father had *plenty of*—was *charm!*

[The scene fades out with music.]

SCENE THREE

Legend on screen: "After the fiasco—" *Tom speaks from the fire escape landing.*

TOM: After the fiasco at Rubicam's Business College, the idea of getting a gentleman caller for Laura began to play a more and more important part in Mother's calculations. It became an obsession. Like some archetype of the universal unconscious, the image of the gentleman caller haunted our small apartment. . . .

[Screen image: A young man at the door of a house with flowers.]

An evening at home rarely passed without some allusion to this image, this specter, this hope. . . . Even when he wasn't mentioned, his presence hung in Mother's preoccupied look and in my sister's frightened, apologetic manner—hung like a sentence passed upon the Wingfields!

Mother was a woman of action as well as words. She began to take logical steps in the planned direction. Late that winter and in the early spring—realizing that extra money would be needed to properly feather the nest and plume the bird—she conducted a vigorous campaign on the telephone, roping in subscribers to one of those magazines for matrons called *The Homemaker's Companion,* the type of journal that features the serialized sublimations of ladies of letters who think in terms of delicate cuplike breasts, slim, tapering waists, rich, creamy thighs, eyes like wood smoke in autumn, fingers that soothe and caress like strains of music, bodies as powerful as Etruscan sculpture.

[Screen image: The cover of a glamour magazine. Amanda enters with the telephone on a long extension cord. She is spotlighted in the dim stage.]

AMANDA: Ida Scott? This is Amanda Wingfield! We *missed* you at the D.A.R. last Monday! I said to myself: She's probably suffering with that sinus condition! How is that sinus condition? Horrors! Heaven have mercy!—You're a Christian martyr, yes, that's what you *telemarketer*

are, a Christian martyr! Well, I just now happened to notice that your subscription to the *Companion*'s about to expire! Yes, it expires with the next issue, honey!—just when that wonderful new serial by Bessie Mae Hopper is getting off to such an exciting start. Oh, honey, it's something that you can't miss! You remember how *Gone with the Wind* took everybody by storm? You simply couldn't go out if you hadn't read it. All everybody *talked* was Scarlett O'Hara. Well, this is a book that critics already compare to *Gone with the Wind*. It's the *Gone with the Wind* of the post-World-War generation! —What? — Burning? —Oh, honey, don't let them burn, go take a look in the oven and I'll hold the wire! Heavens—I think she's hung up!

[*The scene dims out. Legend on screen: "You think I'm in love with Continental Shoemakers?" Before the lights come up again, the violent voices of Tom and Amanda are heard. They are quarreling behind the portieres. In front of them stands Laura with clenched hands and panicky expression. A clear pool of light is on her figure throughout this scene.*]

TOM: What in Christ's name am I—

AMANDA [*shrilly*]: Don't you use that—

TOM: —supposed to do!

AMANDA: —expression! Not in my—

TOM: Ohhh!

AMANDA: —presence! Have you gone out of your senses?

TOM: I have, that's true, *driven* out!

AMANDA: What is the matter with you, you—big—big— IDIOT!

TOM: Look!—I've got *no thing*, no single thing—

AMANDA: Lower your voice!

TOM: —in my life here that I can call my OWN! Everything is—

AMANDA: Stop that shouting!

TOM: Yesterday you confiscated my books! You had the nerve to—

AMANDA: I took that horrible novel back to the library—yes! That hideous book by that insane Mr. Lawrence. [*Tom laughs wildly.*] I cannot control the output of diseased minds or people who cater to them— [*Tom laughs still more wildly.*] BUT I WON'T ALLOW SUCH FILTH BROUGHT INTO MY HOUSE! No, no, no, no, no!

TOM: House, house! Who pays rent on it, who makes a slave of himself to—

AMANDA [*fairly screeching*]: Don't you DARE to—

TOM: No, no, I mustn't say things! *I've* got to just—

AMANDA: Let me tell you—

TOM: I don't want to hear any more!

[*He tears the portieres open. The dining-room area is lit with a turgid smoky red glow. Now we see Amanda; her hair is in metal curlers and she is wearing a very old bathrobe, much too large for her slight figure, a relic of the faithless Mr. Wingfield. The upright typewriter now stands on the drop-leaf table, along with a wild disarray of manuscripts. The quarrel was probably precipitated by Amanda's interruption of Tom's creative labor. A chair lies overthrown on the floor. Their gesticulating shadows are cast on the ceiling by the fiery glow.*]

AMANDA: You *will* hear more, you—

TOM: No, I won't hear more, I'm going out!

AMANDA: You come right back in—

TOM: Out, out, out! Because I'm—

AMANDA: Come back here, Tom Wingfield! I'm not through talking to you!

TOM: Oh, go—

LAURA [*desperately*]: —Tom! *doesn't like their fighting*

AMANDA: You're going to listen, and no more insolence from you! I'm at the end of my patience!

[He comes back toward her.]

TOM: What do you think I'm at? Aren't I supposed to have any patience to reach the end of, Mother? I know, I know. It seems unimportant to you, what I'm *doing*—what I *want* to do—having a little *difference* between them! You don't think that—

AMANDA: I think you've been doing things that you're ashamed of. That's why you act like this. I don't believe that you go every night to the movies. Nobody goes to the movies night after night. Nobody in their right minds goes to the movies as often as you pretend to. People don't go to the movies at nearly midnight, and movies don't let out at two A.M. Come in stumbling. Muttering to yourself like a maniac! You get three hours' sleep and then go to work. Oh, I can picture the way you're doing down there. Moping, doping, because you're in no condition.

TOM [*wildly*]: No, I'm in no condition!   *drinking?*

AMANDA: What right have you got to jeopardize your job? Jeopardize the security of us all? How do you think we'd manage if you were—

TOM: Listen! You think I'm crazy about the *warehouse?* [*He bends fiercely toward her slight figure.*] You think I'm in love with the Continental Shoemakers? You think I want to spend fifty-five *years* down there in that—*celotex interior!* with—*fluorescent—tubes!* Look! I'd rather somebody picked up a crowbar and battered out my brains— than go back mornings! I *go!* Every time you come in yelling that Goddamn *"Rise and Shine!" "Rise and Shine!"* I say to myself, "How *lucky dead* people are!" But I get up. I *go!* For sixty-five dollars a month I give up all that I dream of doing and being *ever!* And you say self—*self's* all I ever think of. Why, listen, if self is what I thought of, Mother, I'd be where he is—GONE! [*He points to his father's picture.*] As far as the system of transportation reaches! [*He starts past her. She grabs his arm.*] Don't grab at me, Mother!

AMANDA: Where are you going?

TOM: I'm going to the *movies!*

AMANDA: I don't believe that lie!

[*Tom crouches toward her, overtowering her tiny figure. She backs away, gasping.*]

sarcasm

TOM: I'm going to opium dens! Yes, opium dens, dens of vice and criminals' hangouts, Mother. I've joined the Hogan Gang, I'm a hired assassin, I carry a tommy gun in a violin case! I run a string of cat houses in the Valley! They call me Killer, Killer Wingfield, I'm leading a double-life, a simple, honest warehouse worker by day, by night a dynamic *czar* of the *underworld, Mother.* I go to gambling casinos, I spin away fortunes on the roulette table! I wear a patch over one eye and a false mustache, sometimes I put on green whiskers. On those occasions they call me—*El Diablo!* Oh, I could tell you many things to make you sleepless! My enemies plan to dynamite this place. They're going to blow us all sky-high some night! I'll be glad, very happy, and so will you! You'll go up, up on a broomstick, over Blue Mountain with seventeen gentlemen callers! You ugly—babbling old—*witch*. . . . [*He goes through a series of violent, clumsy movements, seizing his overcoat, lunging to the door, pulling it fiercely open. The women watch him, aghast. His arm catches in the sleeve of the coat as he struggles to pull it on. For a moment he is pinioned by the bulky garment. With an outraged groan he tears the coat off again, splitting the shoulder of it, and hurls it across the room. It strikes against the shelf of Laura's glass collection, and there is a tinkle of shattering glass. Laura cries out as if wounded.*]

[*Music. Screen legend: "The Glass Menagerie."*]

LAURA [*shrilly*]: My glass!—menagerie. . . . [*She covers her face and turns away.*]

[*But Amanda is still stunned and stupefied by the "ugly witch" so that she barely notices this occurrence. Now she recovers her speech.*]

AMANDA [*in an awful voice*]: I won't speak to you—until you apologize!

[*She crosses through the portieres and draws them together behind her. Tom is left with Laura. Laura clings weakly to the mantel with her face averted. Tom stares at her stupidly for a moment. Then he crosses to the shelf. He drops awkwardly on his knees to collect the fallen glass, glancing at Laura as if he would speak but couldn't. "The Glass Menagerie" music steals in as the scene dims out.]*

SCENE FOUR

The interior of the apartment is dark. There is a faint light in the alley. A deep-voiced bell in a church is tolling the hour of five.

Tom appears at the top of the alley. After each solemn boom of the bell in the tower, he shakes a little noisemaker or rattle as if to express the tiny spasm of man in contrast to the sustained power and dignity of the Almighty. This and the unsteadiness of his advance make it evident that he has been drinking. As he climbs the few steps to the fire escape landing light steals up inside, Laura appears in the front room in a nightdress. She notices that Tom's bed is empty. Tom fishes in his pockets for his door key, removing a motley assortment of articles in the search, including a shower of movie ticket stubs and an empty bottle. At last he finds the key, but just as he is about to insert it, it slips from his fingers. He strikes a match and crouches below the door.

TOM [*bitterly*]: One crack—and it falls through!

[*Laura opens the door.*]

LAURA: Tom! Tom, what are you doing?

TOM: Looking for a door key.

LAURA: Where have you been all this time?

TOM: I have been to the movies.

LAURA: All this time at the movies?

TOM: There was a very long program. There was a Garbo picture and a Mickey Mouse and a travelogue and a newsreel and a preview of coming attractions. And there was an organ solo and a collection for the Milk Fund—simultaneously—which ended up in a terrible fight between a fat lady and an usher!

LAURA [*innocently*]: Did you have to stay through everything?

TOM: Of course! And, oh, I forgot! There was a big stage show! The headliner on this stage show was Malvolio the Magician. He performed wonderful tricks, many of them, such as pouring water back and forth between pitchers. First it turned to wine and then it turned to beer and then it turned to whisky. I know it was whisky it finally turned into because he needed somebody to come up out of the audience to help him, and I came up—both shows! It was Kentucky Straight Bourbon. A very generous fellow, he gave souvenirs. [*He pulls from his back pocket a shimmering rainbow-colored scarf.*] He gave me this. This is his magic scarf. You can have it, Laura. You wave it over a canary cage and you get a bowl of goldfish. You wave it over the goldfish bowl and they fly away canaries. . . . But the wonderfullest trick of all was the coffin trick. We nailed him into a coffin and he got out of the coffin without removing one nail. [*He has come inside.*] There is a trick that would come in handy for me—get me out of this two-by-four situation! [*He flops onto the bed and starts removing his shoes.*]

LAURA: Tom—shhh!

TOM: What're you shushing me for?

LAURA: You'll wake up Mother.

TOM: Goody, goody! Pay 'er back for all those "Rise an' Shines." [*He lies down, groaning.*] You know it don't take much intelligence to get yourself into a nailed-up coffin, Laura. But who in hell ever got himself out of one without removing one nail?

[*As if in answer, the father's grinning photograph lights up. The scene dims out. Immediately following, the church bell is heard striking six. At the sixth stroke the alarm clock goes off in Amanda's room, and after a few moments we hear her calling.*]

AMANDA [*offstage*]: Rise and Shine! Rise and Shine! Laura, go tell your brother to rise and shine!

TOM [*sitting up slowly*]: I'll rise—but I won't shine.

[*The light increases.*]

AMANDA [*offstage*]: Laura, tell your brother his coffee is ready.

[*Laura slips into the front room.*]

LAURA: Tom!—It's nearly seven. Don't make Mother nervous.

[*He stares at her stupidly.*]

[*Beseechingly.*] Tom, speak to Mother this morning. Make up with her, apologize, speak to her!

TOM: She won't to me. It's her that started not speaking.

LAURA: If you just say you're sorry she'll start speaking.

TOM: Her not speaking—is that such a tragedy? *he's very sarcastic*

LAURA: Please—please!

AMANDA [*calling from the kitchenette*]: Laura, are you going to do what I asked you to do, or do I have to get dressed and go out myself?

LAURA: Going, going—soon as I get on my coat! [*She pulls on a shapeless felt hat with a nervous, jerky movement, pleadingly glancing at Tom. She rushes awkwardly for her coat. The coat is one of Amanda's, inaccurately made-over, the sleeves too short for Laura.*] Butter and what else?

AMANDA [*entering from the kitchenette*]: Just butter. Tell them to charge it.

LAURA: Mother, they make such faces when I do that.

AMANDA: Sticks and stones can break our bones, but the expression on Mr. Garfinkel's face won't harm us! Tell your brother his coffee is getting cold.

LAURA [*at the door*]: Do what I asked you, will you, will you, Tom?

[*He looks sullenly away.*]

AMANDA: Laura, go now or just don't go at all!

LAURA [*rushing out*]: Going—going!

[*A second later she cries out. Tom springs up and crosses to the door. Tom opens the door.*]

TOM: Laura?

LAURA: I'm all right. I slipped, but I'm all right.

AMANDA [*peering anxiously after her*]: If anyone breaks a leg on those fire-escape steps, the landlord ought to be sued for every cent he possesses! [*She shuts the door. Now she remembers she isn't speaking to Tom and returns to the other room.*]

[*As Tom comes listlessly for his coffee, she turns her back to him and stands rigidly facing the window on the gloomy gray vault of the areaway, its light on her face with its aged but childish features is cruelly sharp, satirical as a Daumier print. The music of "Ave Maria," is heard softly. Tom glances sheepishly but sullenly at her averted figure and slumps at the table. The coffee is scalding hot; he sips it and gasps and spits it back in the cup. At his gasp, Amanda catches her breath and half turns. Then she catches herself and turns back to the window. Tom blows on his coffee, glancing sidewise at his mother. She clears her throat. Tom clears his. He starts to rise, sinks back down again, scratches his head, clears his throat again. Amanda coughs. Tom raises his cup in both hands to blow on it, his eyes staring over the rim of it at his mother for several moments. Then he slowly sets the cup down and awkwardly and hesitantly rises from the chair.*]

TOM [*hoarsely*]: Mother. I—I apologize, Mother.

[*Amanda draws a quick, shuddering breath. Her face works grotesquely. She breaks into childlike tears.*]

I'm sorry for what I said, for everything that I said, I didn't mean it.

AMANDA [*sobbingly*]: My devotion has made me a witch and so I make myself hateful to my children!

TOM: *No, you don't.*

AMANDA: I worry so much, don't sleep, it makes me nervous!

TOM [*gently*]: I understand that.

AMANDA: I've had to put up a solitary battle all these years. But you're my right-hand bower! Don't fall down, don't fail!

TOM [*gently*]: I try, Mother.

AMANDA [*with great enthusiasm*]: Try and you will *succeed!* [*The notion makes her breathless.*] Why, you—you're just *full* of natural endowments! Both of my children—they're *unusual* children! Don't you think I know it? I'm so—*proud!* Happy and—feel I've—so much to be thankful for but—promise me one thing, son!

TOM: What, Mother?

AMANDA: Promise, son, you'll—never be a drunkard!

TOM [*turns to her grinning*]: I will never be a drunkard, Mother.

AMANDA: That's what frightened me so, that you'd be drinking! Eat a bowl of Purina!

yikes

TOM: Just coffee, Mother.

AMANDA: Shredded wheat biscuit?

TOM: No. No, Mother, just coffee.

AMANDA: You can't put in a day's work on an empty stomach. You've got ten minutes—don't gulp! Drinking too-hot liquids makes cancer of the stomach. . . . Put cream in.

TOM: No, thank you.

AMANDA: To cool it.

TOM: No! No, thank you, I want it black.

AMANDA: I know, but it's not good for you. We have to do all that we can to build ourselves up. In these trying times we live in, all that we have to cling to is—each other. . . . That's why it's so important to— Tom, I— I sent out your sister so I could discuss something with you. If you hadn't spoken I would have spoken to you. [*She sits down.*]

TOM [*gently*]: What is it, Mother, that you want to discuss?

AMANDA: *Laura!*

[*Tom puts his cup down slowly. Legend on screen: "Laura." Music: "The Glass Menagerie."*]

TOM: —Oh. —Laura . . .

AMANDA [*touching his sleeve*]: You know how Laura is. So quiet but—still water runs deep! She notices things and I think she—broods about them.

[*Tom looks up.*]

A few days ago I came in and she was crying.

TOM: What about?

AMANDA: You.

TOM: Me?

AMANDA: She has an idea that you're not happy here.

TOM: What gave her that idea?

AMANDA: What gives her any idea? However, you do act strangely. I—I'm not criticizing, understand *that!* I know your ambitions do not lie in the warehouse, that like everybody in the whole wide world— you've had to—make sacrifices, but—Tom—Tom—life's not easy, it calls for—Spartan endurance! There's so many things in my heart that I cannot describe to you! I've never told you but I—*loved* your father. . . .

TOM [*gently*]: I know that, Mother.

AMANDA: And you—when I see you taking after his ways! Staying out late—and—well, you *had* been drinking the night you were in that—terrifying condition! Laura says that you hate the apartment and that you go out nights to get away from it! Is that true, Tom?

TOM: No. You say there's so much in your heart that you can't describe to me. That's true of me, too. There's so much in my heart that I can't describe to *you!* So let's respect each other's—

AMANDA: But, why—*why,* Tom—are you always so *restless?* Where do you *go* to, nights?

TOM: I—go to the movies.

AMANDA: Why do you go to the movies so much, Tom?

TOM: I go to the movies because—I like adventure. Adventure is something I don't have much of at work, so I go to the movies.

AMANDA: But, Tom, you go to the movies *entirely* too *much!*

TOM: I like a lot of adventure. → knows he's lying

[*Amanda looks baffled, then hurt. As the familiar inquisition resumes, Tom becomes hard and impatient again. Amanda slips back into her querulous attitude toward him. Image on screen: A sailing vessel with Jolly Roger.*]

AMANDA: Most young men find adventure in their careers.

TOM: Then most young men are not employed in a warehouse.

AMANDA: The world is full of young men employed in warehouses and offices and factories.

TOM: Do all of them find adventure in their careers?

AMANDA: They do or they do without it! Not everybody has a craze for adventure.

TOM: Man is by instinct a lover, a hunter, a fighter, and none of those instincts are given much play at the warehouse!

AMANDA: Man is by instinct! Don't quote instinct to me! Instinct is something that people have got away from! It belongs to animals! Christian adults don't want it!

TOM: What do Christian adults want, then, Mother?

AMANDA: Superior things! Things of the mind and the spirit! Only animals have to satisfy instincts! Surely your aims are somewhat higher than theirs! Than monkeys—pigs—

TOM: I reckon they're not.

AMANDA: You're joking. However, that isn't what I wanted to discuss.

TOM [*rising*]: I haven't much time.

AMANDA [*pushing his shoulders*]: Sit down.

TOM: You want me to punch in red at the warehouse, Mother?

AMANDA: You have five minutes. I want to talk about Laura.

[Screen legend: "Plans and Provisions."]

TOM: All right! What about Laura?

AMANDA: We have to be making some plans and provisions for her. She's older than you, two years, and nothing has happened. She just drifts along doing nothing. It frightens me terribly how she just drifts along.

TOM: I guess she's the type that people call home girls.

AMANDA: There's no such type, and if there is, it's a pity! That is unless the home is hers, with a husband!

TOM: What?

AMANDA: Oh, I can see the handwriting on the wall as plain as I see the nose in front of my face! It's terrifying! More and more you remind me of your father! He was out all hours without explanation!— Then *left! Goodbye!* And me with the bag to hold. I saw that letter you got from the Merchant Marine. I know what you're dreaming of. I'm not standing here blindfolded. [*She pauses.*] Very well, then. Then *do* it! But not till there's somebody to take your place. *wants to leave*

TOM: What do you mean?

AMANDA: I mean that as soon as Laura has got somebody to take care of her, married, a home of her own, independent—why, then you'll be free to go wherever you please, on land, on sea, whichever way the wind blows you! But until that time you've got to look out for your sister. I don't say me because I'm old and don't matter! I say for your sister because she's young and dependent.

I put her in business college—a dismal failure! Frightened her so it made her sick at the stomach. I took her over to the Young People's League at the church. Another fiasco. She spoke to nobody, nobody spoke to her. Now all she does is fool with those pieces of glass and play those worn-out records. What kind of a life is that for a girl to lead?

TOM: What can I do about it?

AMANDA: Overcome selfishness! Self, self, self is all that you ever think of!

[*Tom springs up and crosses to get his coat. It is ugly and bulky. He pulls on a cap with earmuffs.*]

Where is your muffler? Put your wool muffler on!

[*He snatches it angrily from the closet, tosses it around his neck and pulls both ends tight.*]

Tom! I haven't said what I had in mind to ask you.

TOM: I'm too late to—

AMANDA [*catching his arm—very importunately; then shyly*]: Down at the warehouse, aren't there some—nice young men?

TOM: No!

AMANDA: There *must* be—*some* . . .

TOM: Mother— [*He gestures.*]

AMANDA: Find out one that's clean-living—doesn't drink and ask him out for sister!

TOM: What?

AMANDA: For *sister!* To *meet!* Get *acquainted!*

TOM [*stamping to the door*]: Oh, my go-osh!

AMANDA: Will you?

[*He opens the door. She says, imploringly:*]

Will you?

[*He starts down the fire escape.*]

Will you? *Will* you, dear?

TOM [*calling back*]: Yes!

[Amanda closes the door hesitantly and with a troubled but faintly hopeful expression. Screen image: The cover of a glamour magazine. The spotlight picks up Amanda at the phone.]

AMANDA: Ella Cartwright? This is Amanda Wingfield! How are you, honey? How is that kidney condition? [*There is a five-second pause.*] Horrors! [*There is another pause.*] You're a Christian martyr, yes, honey, that's what you are, a Christian martyr! Well, I just now happened to notice in my little red book that your subscription to the *Companion* has just run out! I knew that you wouldn't want to miss out on the wonderful serial starting in this new issue. It's by Bessie Mae Hopper, the first thing she's written since *Honeymoon for Three*. Wasn't that a strange and interesting story? Well, this one is even lovelier, I believe. It has a sophisticated, society background. It's all about the horsey set on Long Island!

[The light fades out.]

SCENE FIVE

Legend on the screen: "Annunciation." *Music is heard as the light slowly comes on. It is early dusk of a spring evening. Supper has just been finished in the Wingfield apartment. Amanda and Laura, in light-colored dresses, are removing dishes from the table in the dining room, which is shadowy, their movements formalized almost as a dance or ritual, their moving forms as pale and silent as moths. Tom, in white shirt and trousers, rises from the table and crosses toward the fire escape.*

AMANDA [*as he passes her*]: Son, will you do me a favor?

TOM: What?

AMANDA: Comb your hair! You look so pretty when your hair is combed!

[*Tom slouches on the sofa with the evening paper. Its enormous headline reads: "Franco Triumphs."*]

There is only one respect in which I would like you to emulate your father.

TOM: What respect is that?

AMANDA: The care he always took of his appearance. He never allowed himself to look untidy.

[*He throws down the paper and crosses to the fire escape.*]

Where are you going?

TOM: I'm going out to smoke.

AMANDA: You smoke too much. A pack a day at fifteen cents a pack. How much would that amount to in a month? Thirty times fifteen is how much, Tom? Figure it out and you will be astounded at what you could save. Enough to give you a night-school course in accounting at Washington U.! Just think what a wonderful thing that would be for you, son!

go to college

46

[*Tom is unmoved by the thought.*]

TOM: I'd rather smoke. [*He steps out on the landing, letting the screen door slam.*]

AMANDA [*sharply*]: I know! That's the tragedy of it. . . . [*Alone, she turns to look at her husband's picture.*]

[*Dance music: "The World Is Waiting for the Sunrise!"*]

TOM [*to the audience*]: Across the alley from us was the Paradise Dance Hall. On evenings in spring the windows and doors were open and the music came outdoors. Sometimes the lights were turned out except for a large glass sphere that hung from the ceiling. It would turn slowly about and filter the dusk with delicate rainbow colors. Then the orchestra played a waltz or a tango, something that had a slow and sensuous rhythm. Couples would come outside, to the relative privacy of the alley. You could see them kissing behind ash pits and telephone poles. This was the compensation for lives that passed like mine, without any change or adventure. Adventure and change were imminent in this year. They were waiting around the corner for all these kids. Suspended in the mist over Berchtesgaden, caught in the folds of Chamberlain's umbrella. In Spain there was Guernica! But here there was only hot swing music and liquor, dance halls, bars, and movies, and sex that hung in the gloom like a chandelier and flooded the world with brief, deceptive rainbows. . . . All the world was waiting for bombardments!

[*Amanda turns from the picture and comes outside.*]

AMANDA [*sighing*]: A fire escape landing's a poor excuse for a porch. [*She spreads a newspaper on a step and sits down, gracefully and demurely as if she were settling into a swing on a Mississippi veranda.*] What are you looking at?

TOM: The moon.

AMANDA: Is there a moon this evening?

TOM: It's rising over Garfinkel's Delicatessen.

AMANDA: So it is! A little silver slipper of a moon. Have you made a wish on it yet?

TOM: Um-hum.

AMANDA: What did you wish for?

TOM: That's a secret.

AMANDA: A secret, huh? Well, I won't tell mine either. I will be just as mysterious as you.

TOM: I bet I can guess what yours is.

AMANDA: Is my head so transparent?

TOM: You're not a sphinx.

AMANDA: No, I don't have secrets. I'll tell you what I wished for on the moon. Success and happiness for my precious children! I wish for that whenever there's a moon, and when there isn't a moon, I wish for it, too.

TOM: I thought perhaps you wished for a gentleman caller.

AMANDA: Why do you say that?

TOM: Don't you remember asking me to fetch one?

AMANDA: I remember suggesting that it would be nice for your sister if you brought home some nice young man from the warehouse. I think that I've made that suggestion more than once.

TOM: Yes, you have made it repeatedly.

AMANDA: Well?

TOM: We are going to have one.

AMANDA: *What?*

TOM: A gentleman caller!

[*The annunciation is celebrated with music. Amanda rises. Image on screen: A caller with a bouquet.*]

AMANDA: You mean you have asked some nice young man to come over?

TOM: Yep. I've asked him to dinner.

AMANDA: You really did?

TOM: I did!

AMANDA: You did, and did he—*accept?*

TOM: He did!

AMANDA: Well, well—well, well! That's—lovely!

TOM: I thought that you would be pleased.

AMANDA: It's definite then?

TOM: Very definite.

AMANDA: Soon?

TOM: Very soon.

AMANDA: For heaven's sake, stop putting on and tell me some things, will you?

TOM: What things do you want me to tell you?

AMANDA: *Naturally* I would like to know when he's *coming!*

TOM: He's coming tomorrow.

AMANDA: *Tomorrow?*

TOM: Yep. Tomorrow.

AMANDA: But, Tom!

TOM: Yes, Mother?

AMANDA: Tomorrow gives me no time!

TOM: Time for what?

AMANDA: Preparations! Why didn't you phone me at once, as soon as you asked him, the minute that he accepted? Then, don't you see, I could have been getting ready!

TOM: You don't have to make any fuss.

AMANDA: Oh, Tom, Tom, Tom, of course I have to make a fuss! I want things nice, not sloppy! Not thrown together. I'll certainly have to do some fast thinking, won't I?

TOM: I don't see why you have to think at all.

AMANDA: You just don't know. We can't have a gentleman caller in a pigsty! All my wedding silver has to be polished, the monogrammed table linen ought to be laundered! The windows have to be washed and fresh curtains put up. And how about clothes? We have to *wear* something, don't we?

TOM: Mother, this boy is no one to make a fuss over!

AMANDA: Do you realize he's the first young man we've introduced to your sister? It's terrible, dreadful, disgraceful that poor little sister has never received a single gentleman caller! Tom, come inside! [*She opens the screen door.*]

TOM: What for?

AMANDA: I want to ask you some things.

TOM: If you're going to make such a fuss, I'll call it off, I'll tell him not to come!

AMANDA: You certainly won't do anything of the kind. Nothing offends people worse than broken engagements. It simply means I'll have to work like a Turk! We won't be brilliant, but we will pass inspection. Come on inside.

[*Tom follows her inside, groaning.*]

Sit down.

TOM: Any particular place you would like me to sit?

AMANDA: Thank heavens I've got that new sofa! I'm also making payments on a floor lamp I'll have sent out! And put the chintz covers on, they'll brighten things up! Of course I'd hoped to have these walls re-papered. . . . What is the young man's name?

TOM: His name is O'Connor.

AMANDA: That, of course, means fish—tomorrow is Friday! I'll have that salmon loaf—with Durkee's dressing! What does he do? He works at the warehouse?

TOM: Of course! How else would I—

AMANDA: Tom, he—doesn't drink?

TOM: Why do you ask me that?

AMANDA: Your father *did!*

TOM: Don't get started on that!

AMANDA: He *does* drink, then?

TOM: Not that I know of!

AMANDA: Make sure, be certain! The last thing I want for my daughter's a boy who drinks!

TOM: Aren't you being a little bit premature? Mr. O'Connor has not yet appeared on the scene!

AMANDA: But will tomorrow. To meet your sister, and what do I know about his character? Nothing! Old maids are better off than wives of drunkards! ← reminds him of her husband

TOM: Oh, my God!

AMANDA: Be still!

TOM [*leaning forward to whisper*]: Lots of fellows meet girls whom they don't marry!

AMANDA: Oh, talk sensibly, Tom—and don't be sarcastic! [*She has gotten a hairbrush.*]

TOM: What are you doing?

AMANDA: I'm brushing that cowlick down! [*She attacks his hair with the brush.*] What is this young man's position at the warehouse?

TOM [*submitting grimly to the brush and the interrogation*]: This young man's position is that of a shipping clerk, Mother.

AMANDA: Sounds to me like a fairly responsible job, the sort of a job *you* would be in if you just had more *get-up*. What is his salary? Have you any idea?

TOM: I would judge it to be approximately eighty-five dollars a month.

AMANDA: Well—not princely, but—

TOM: Twenty more than I make.

AMANDA: Yes, how well I know! But for a family man, eighty-five dollars a month is not much more than you can just get by on. . . .

TOM: Yes, but Mr. O'Connor is not a family man.

AMANDA: He might be, mightn't he? Some time in the future?

TOM: I see. Plans and provisions.

AMANDA: You are the only young man that I know of who ignores the fact that the future becomes the present, the present the past, and the past turns into everlasting regret if you don't plan for it!

TOM: I will think that over and see what I can make of it.

AMANDA: Don't be supercilious with your mother! Tell me some more about this—what do you call him?

TOM: James D. O'Connor. The D. is for Delaney.

AMANDA: Irish on *both* sides! *Gracious!* And doesn't drink?

TOM: Shall I call him up and ask him right this minute?

AMANDA: The only way to find out about those things is to make discreet inquiries at the proper moment. When I was a girl in Blue Mountain and it was suspected that a young man drank, the girl whose attentions he had been receiving, if any girl *was,* would sometimes speak to the minister of his church, or rather her father would if her father was living, and sort of feel him out on the young man's character. That is the way such things are discreetly handled to keep a young woman from making a tragic mistake!

TOM: Then how did you happen to make a tragic mistake?

AMANDA: That innocent look of your father's had everyone fooled! He *smiled*—the world was *enchanted!* No girl can do worse than put herself at the mercy of a handsome appearance! I hope that Mr. O'Connor is not too good-looking.

TOM: No, he's not too good-looking. He's covered with freckles and hasn't too much of a nose.

AMANDA: He's not right-down homely, though?

TOM: Not right-down homely. Just medium homely, I'd say.

AMANDA: Character's what to look for in a man.

TOM: That's what I've always said, Mother.

AMANDA: You've never said anything of the kind and I suspect you would never give it a thought.

TOM: Don't be so suspicious of me.

AMANDA: At least I hope he's the type that's up and coming.

TOM: I think he really goes in for self-improvement.

AMANDA: What reason have you to think so?

TOM: He goes to night school.

AMANDA [*beaming*]: Splendid! What does he do, I mean study?

TOM: Radio engineering and public speaking!

AMANDA: Then he has visions of being advanced in the world! Any young man who studies public speaking is aiming to have an executive job some day! And radio engineering? A thing for the future! Both of these facts are very illuminating. Those are the sort of things that a mother should know concerning any young man who comes to call on her daughter. Seriously or—not.

TOM: One little warning. He doesn't know about Laura. I didn't let on that we had dark ulterior motives. I just said, why don't you come and have dinner with us? He said okay and that was the whole conversation. *he def likes him → maybe his secret way of introducing him to the family*

AMANDA: I bet it was! You're eloquent as an oyster. However, he'll know about Laura when he gets here. When he sees how lovely and sweet and pretty she is, he'll thank his lucky stars he was asked to dinner.

TOM: Mother, you mustn't expect too much of Laura.

AMANDA: What do you mean?

TOM: Laura seems all those things to you and me because she's ours and we love her. We don't even notice she's crippled any more.

AMANDA: Don't say crippled! You know that I never allow that word to be used!

TOM: But face facts, Mother. She is and—that's not all—

AMANDA: What do you mean "not all"?

TOM: Laura is very different from other girls.

AMANDA: I think the difference is all to her advantage.

TOM: Not quite all—in the eyes of others—strangers—she's terribly shy and lives in a world of her own and those things make her seem a little peculiar to people outside the house.

AMANDA: Don't say peculiar.

TOM: Face the facts. She is.

[*The dance hall music changes to a tango that has a minor and somewhat ominous tone.*]

AMANDA: In what way is she peculiar—may I ask?

TOM [*gently*]: She lives in a world of her own—a world of little glass ornaments, Mother. . . . [*He gets up. Amanda remains holding the brush, looking at him, troubled.*] She plays old phonograph records and—that's about all— [*He glances at himself in the mirror and crosses to the door.*]

AMANDA [*sharply*]: Where are you going?

TOM: I'm going to the movies. [*He goes out the screen door.*]

AMANDA: Not to the movies, every night to the movies! [*She follows quickly to the screen door.*] I don't believe you always go to the movies!

[*He is gone. Amanda looks worriedly after him for a moment. Then vitality and optimism return and she turns from the door, crossing to the portieres.*]

Laura! Laura!

[*Laura answers from the kitchenette.*]

LAURA: Yes, Mother.

AMANDA: Let those dishes go and come in front!

[*Laura appears with a dish towel. Amanda speaks to her gaily.*]

Laura, come here and make a wish on the moon!

[*Screen image: The Moon.*]

LAURA [*entering*]: Moon—moon?

AMANDA: A little silver slipper of a moon. Look over your left shoulder, Laura, and make a wish!

[*Laura looks faintly puzzled as if called out of sleep. Amanda seizes her shoulders and turns her at an angle by the door.*]

Now! Now, darling, *wish!*

LAURA: What shall I wish for, Mother?

AMANDA [*her voice trembling and her eyes suddenly filling with tears*]: Happiness! Good fortune!

[*The sound of the violin rises and the stage dims out.*]

SCENE SIX

The light comes up on the fire escape landing. Tom is leaning against the grill, smoking. Screen image: The high school hero.

TOM: And so the following evening I brought Jim home to dinner. I had known Jim slightly in high school. In high school Jim was a hero. He had tremendous Irish good nature and vitality with the scrubbed and polished look of white chinaware. He seemed to move in a continual spotlight. He was a star in basketball, captain of the debating club, president of the senior class and the glee club and he sang the male lead in the annual light operas. He was always running or bounding, never just walking. He seemed always at the point of defeating the law of gravity. He was shooting with such velocity through his adolescence that you would logically expect him to arrive at nothing short of the White House by the time he was thirty. But Jim apparently ran into more interference after his graduation from Soldan. His speed had definitely slowed. Six years after he left high school he was holding a job that wasn't much better than mine.

[Screen image: The Clerk.]

He was the only one at the warehouse with whom I was on friendly terms. I was valuable to him as someone who could remember his former glory, who had seen him win basketball games and the silver cup in debating. He knew of my secret practice of retiring to a cabinet of the washroom to work on poems when business was slack in the warehouse. He called me Shakespeare. And while the other boys in the warehouse regarded me with suspicious hostility, Jim took a humorous attitude toward me. Gradually his attitude affected the others, their hostility wore off and they also began to smile at me as people smile at an oddly fashioned dog who trots across their path at some distance.

I knew that Jim and Laura had known each other at Soldan, and I had heard Laura speak admiringly of his voice. I didn't know if Jim remembered her or not. In high school Laura had been as unobtrusive

Omg is this the boy

56

as Jim had been astonishing. If he did remember Laura, it was not as my sister, for when I asked him to dinner, he grinned and said, "You know, Shakespeare, I never thought of you as having folks!"

He was about to discover that I did. . . .

[Legend on screen: "The accent of a coming foot." The light dims out on Tom and comes up in the Wingfield living room—a delicate lemony light. It is about five on a Friday evening of late spring which comes "scattering poems in the sky."

Amanda has worked like a Turk in preparation for the gentleman caller. The results are astonishing. The new floor lamp with its rose silk shade is in place, a colored paper lantern conceals the broken light fixture in the ceiling, new billowing white curtains are at the windows, chintz covers are on the chairs and sofa, a pair of new sofa pillows make their initial appearance. Open boxes and tissue paper are scattered on the floor.

Laura stands in the middle of the room with lifted arms while Amanda crouches before her, adjusting the hem of a new dress, devout and ritualistic. The dress is colored and designed by memory. The arrangement of Laura's hair is changed; it is softer and more becoming. A fragile, unearthly prettiness has come out in Laura: she is like a piece of translucent glass touched by light, given a momentary radiance, not actual, not lasting.]

AMANDA [*impatiently*]: Why are you trembling?

LAURA: Mother, you've made me so nervous!

AMANDA: How have I made you nervous?

LAURA: By all this fuss! You make it seem so important!

AMANDA: I don't understand you, Laura. You couldn't be satisfied with just sitting home, and yet whenever I try to arrange something for you, you seem to resist it. [*She gets up.*] Now take a look at yourself. No, wait! Wait just a moment—I have an idea!

LAURA: What is it now?

[Amanda produces two powder puffs which she wraps in handkerchiefs and stuffs in Laura's bosom.]

LAURA: Mother, what are you doing?

AMANDA: They call them "Gay Deceivers"!

LAURA: I won't wear them!

AMANDA: You will!

LAURA: Why should I?

AMANDA: Because, to be painfully honest, your chest is flat.

LAURA: You make it seem like we were setting a trap.

AMANDA: All pretty girls are a trap, a pretty trap, and men expect them to be.

[Legend on screen: "A pretty trap."]

Now look at yourself, young lady. This is the prettiest you will ever be! *[She stands back to admire Laura.]* I've got to fix myself now! You're going to be surprised by your mother's appearance!

[Amanda crosses through the portieres, humming gaily. Laura moves slowly to the long mirror and stares solemnly at herself. A wind blows the white curtains inward in a slow, graceful motion and with a faint, sorrowful sighing.]

AMANDA *[from somewhere behind the portieres]*: It isn't dark enough yet.

[Laura turns slowly before the mirror with a troubled look. Legend on screen: "This is my sister: Celebrate her with strings!" Music plays.]

AMANDA *[laughing, still not visible]*: I'm going to show you something. I'm going to make a spectacular appearance!

LAURA: What is it, Mother?

AMANDA: Possess your soul in patience—you will see! Something I've resurrected from that old trunk! Styles haven't changed so terribly much after all. . . . *[She parts the portieres.]* Now just look at your mother! *[She wears a girlish frock of yellowed voile with a blue*

silk sash. She carries a bunch of jonquils—the legend of her youth is **lives through Laura** **trying to stay in the past**
nearly revived. Now she speaks feverishly.] This is the dress in which
I led the cotillion. Won the Cakewalk twice at Sunset Hill, wore one
Spring to the Governor's Ball in Jackson! See how I sashayed around
the ballroom, Laura? [*She raises her skirt and does a mincing step
around the room.*] I wore it on Sundays for my gentlemen callers! I had
it on the day I met your father. . . . I had malaria fever all that Spring.
The change of climate from East Tennessee to the Delta—weakened
resistance. I had a little temperature all the time—not enough to be serious—just enough to make me restless and giddy! Invitations poured
in—parties all over the Delta! "Stay in bed," said Mother, "you have a
fever!"—but I just wouldn't. I took quinine but kept on going, going!
Evenings, dances! Afternoons, long, long rides! Picnics—lovely! So
lovely, that country in May—all lacy with dogwood, literally flooded
with jonquils! That was the spring I had the craze for jonquils. Jonquils became an absolute obsession. Mother said, "Honey, there's no
more room for jonquils." And still I kept on bringing in more jonquils.
Whenever, wherever I saw them, I'd say, "Stop! Stop! I see jonquils!"
I made the young men help me gather the jonquils! It was a joke,
Amanda and her jonquils. Finally there were no more vases to hold
them, every available space was filled with jonquils. No vases to hold
them? All right, I'll hold them myself! And then I— [*She stops in
front of the picture. Music plays.*] met your father! Malaria fever and
jonquils and then—this—boy. . . . [*She switches on the rose-colored
lamp.*] I hope they get here before it starts to rain. [*She crosses the
room and places the jonquils in a bowl on the table.*] I gave your
brother a little extra change so he and Mr. O'Connor could take the
service car home.

LAURA [*with an altered look*]: What did you say his name was?

AMANDA: O'Connor.

LAURA: What is his first name?

AMANDA: I don't remember. Oh, yes, I do. It was—Jim!

[*Laura sways slightly and catches hold of a chair. Legend on screen:
"Not Jim!"*]

LAURA [*faintly*]: Not—Jim!

AMANDA: Yes, that was it, it was Jim! I've never known a Jim that wasn't nice!

[*The music becomes ominous.*]

LAURA: Are you sure his name is Jim O'Connor?

AMANDA: Yes. Why?

LAURA: Is he the one that Tom used to know in high school?

AMANDA: He didn't say so. I think he just got to know him at the warehouse.

LAURA: There was a Jim O'Connor we both knew in high school— [*Then, with effort.*] If that is the one that Tom is bringing to dinner— you'll have to excuse me, I won't come to the table.

AMANDA: What sort of nonsense is this?

LAURA: You asked me once if I'd ever liked a boy. Don't you re- member I showed you this boy's picture?

AMANDA: You mean the boy you showed me in the yearbook?

LAURA: Yes, that boy.

AMANDA: Laura, Laura, were you in love with that boy?

LAURA: I don't know, Mother. All I know is I couldn't sit at the table if it was him!

AMANDA: It won't be him! It isn't the least bit likely. But whether it is or not, you will come to the table. You will not be excused.

LAURA: I'll have to be, Mother.

AMANDA: I don't intend to humor your silliness, Laura. I've had too much from you and your brother, both! So just sit down and com- pose yourself till they come. Tom has forgotten his key so you'll have to let them in, when they arrive.

LAURA [*panicky*]: Oh, Mother—*you* answer the door!

AMANDA [*lightly*]: I'll be in the kitchen—busy!

LAURA: Oh, Mother, please answer the door, don't make me do it!

AMANDA [*crossing into the kitchenette*]: I've got to fix the dressing for the salmon. Fuss, fuss—silliness!—over a gentleman caller!

[*The door swings shut. Laura is left alone. Legend on screen: "Terror!" She utters a low moan and turns off the lamp—sits stiffly on the edge of the sofa, knotting her fingers together.*]

  Legend on screen: "The Opening of a Door!" Tom and Jim appear on the fire escape steps and climb to the landing. Hearing their approach, Laura rises with a panicky gesture. She retreats to the portieres. The doorbell rings. Laura catches her breath and touches her throat. Low drums sound.]

AMANDA [*calling*]: Laura, sweetheart! The door!

[*Laura stares at it without moving.*]

JIM: I think we just beat the rain.

TOM: Uh-huh. [*He rings again, nervously. Jim whistles and fishes for a cigarette.*]

AMANDA [*very, very gaily*]: Laura, that is your brother and Mr. O'Connor! Will you let them in, darling?

[*Laura crosses toward the kitchenette door.*]

LAURA [*breathlessly*]: Mother—you go to the door!

[*Amanda steps out of the kitchenette and stares furiously at Laura. She points imperiously at the door.*]

Please, please!

AMANDA [*in a fierce whisper*]: What is the matter with you, you silly thing?

LAURA [*desperately*]: Please, you answer it, please!

AMANDA: I told you I wasn't going to humor you, Laura. Why have you chosen this moment to lose your mind?

LAURA: Please, please, please, you go!

AMANDA: You'll have to go to the door because I can't!

LAURA [*despairingly*]: I can't either!

AMANDA: *Why?*

LAURA: I'm *sick!*

AMANDA: I'm sick, too—of your nonsense! Why can't you and your brother be normal people? Fantastic whims and behavior! [*Tom gives a long ring.*] Preposterous goings on! Can you give me one reason— [*She calls out lyrically.*] *Coming! Just one second!*—why you should be afraid to open a door? Now you answer it, Laura!

LAURA: Oh, oh, oh . . . [*She returns through the portieres, darts to the Victrola, winds it frantically and turns it on.*]

AMANDA: Laura Wingfield, you march right to that door!

LAURA: *Yes—yes, Mother!*

[*A faraway, scratchy rendition of "Dardanella" softens the air and gives her strength to move through it. She slips to the door and draws it cautiously open. Tom enters with the caller, Jim O'Connor.*]

TOM: Laura, this is Jim. Jim, this is my sister, Laura.

JIM [*stepping inside*]: I didn't know that Shakespeare had a sister!

LAURA [*retreating, stiff and trembling, from the door*]: How—how do you do?

JIM [*heartily, extending his hand*]: Okay!

[*Laura touches it hesitantly with hers.*]

JIM: Your hand's *cold*, Laura!

LAURA: Yes, well—I've been playing the Victrola. . . .

JIM: Must have been playing classical music on it! You ought to play a little hot swing music to warm you up!

LAURA: Excuse me—I haven't finished playing the Victrola. . . . [*She turns awkwardly and hurries into the front room. She pauses a second by the Victrola. Then she catches her breath and darts through the portieres like a frightened deer.*]

JIM [*grinning*]: What was the matter?

TOM: Oh—with Laura? Laura is—terribly shy.

JIM: Shy, huh? It's unusual to meet a shy girl nowadays. I don't believe you ever mentioned you had a sister.

TOM: Well, now you know. I have one. Here is the *Post Dispatch.* You want a piece of it?

JIM: Uh-huh.

TOM: What piece? The comics?

JIM: Sports! [*He glances at it.*] Ole Dizzy Dean is on his bad behavior

TOM [*uninterested*]: Yeah? [*He lights a cigarette and goes over to the fire-escape door.*]

JIM: Where are *you* going?

TOM: I'm going out on the terrace.

JIM [*going after him*]: You know, Shakespeare—I'm going to sell you a bill of goods!

TOM: What goods?

JIM: A course I'm taking.

TOM: Huh?

JIM: In public speaking! You and me, we're not the warehouse type.

TOM: Thanks—that's good news. But what has public speaking got to do with it?

JIM: It fits you for—executive positions!

look flirty

TOM: Awww.

JIM: I tell you it's done a helluva lot for me.

[Image on screen: Executive at his desk.]

TOM: In what respect?

JIM: In every! Ask yourself what is the difference between you an' me and men in the office down front? Brains?— No!— Ability?— No! Then what? Just one little thing—

TOM: What is that one little thing?

JIM: Primarily it amounts to—social poise! Being able to square up to people and hold your own on any social level!

AMANDA *[from the kitchenette]*: Tom?

TOM: Yes, Mother?

AMANDA: Is that you and Mr. O'Connor?

TOM: Yes, Mother.

AMANDA: Well, you just make yourselves comfortable in there.

TOM: Yes, Mother.

AMANDA: Ask Mr. O'Connor if he would like to wash his hands.

JIM: Aw, no—no—thank you—I took care of that at the warehouse. Tom—

TOM: Yes?

JIM: Mr. Mendoza was speaking to me about you.

TOM: Favorably?

JIM: What do you think?

TOM: Well—

JIM: You're going to be out of a job if you don't wake up.

TOM: I am waking up—

JIM: You show no signs.

TOM: The signs are interior.

[*Image on screen: The sailing vessel with the Jolly Roger again.*]

TOM: I'm planning to change. [*He leans over the fire escape rail, speaking with quiet exhilaration. The incandescent marquees and signs of the first-run movie houses light his face from across the alley. He looks like a voyager.*] I'm right at the point of committing myself to a future that doesn't include the warehouse and Mr. Mendoza or even a night-school course in public speaking. *he's the point*

JIM: What are you gassing about?

TOM: I'm tired of the movies.

JIM: Movies!

TOM: Yes, movies! Look at them— [*A wave toward the marvels of Grand Avenue.*] All of those glamorous people—having adventures—hogging it all, gobbling the whole thing up! You know what happens? People go to the *movies* instead of *moving!* Hollywood characters are supposed to have all the adventures for everybody in America, while everybody in America sits in a dark room and watches them have them! Yes, until there's a war. That's when adventure becomes available to the masses! *Everyone's* dish, not only Gable's! Then the people in the dark room come out of the dark room to have some adventures themselves—goody, goody! It's our turn now, to go to the South Sea Island—to make a safari—to be exotic, far-off! But I'm not patient. I don't want to wait till then. I'm tired of the *movies* and I am *about* to *move!* *tangent*

JIM [*incredulously*]: Move?

TOM: Yes.

JIM: When?

TOM: Soon!

JIM: Where? Where? *doesn't want him to -* 🖊

[The music seems to answer the question, while Tom thinks it over. He searches in his pockets.]

TOM: I'm starting to boil inside. I know I seem dreamy, but inside—well, I'm boiling! Whenever I pick up a shoe, I shudder a little thinking how short life is and what I am doing! Whatever that means, I know it doesn't mean shoes—except as something to wear on a traveler's feet! *[He finds what be has been searching for in his pockets and holds out a paper to Jim.]* Look—

JIM: What?

TOM: I'm a member.

JIM *[reading]*: The Union of Merchant Seamen.

TOM: I paid my dues this month, instead of the light bill.

JIM: You will regret it when they turn the lights off.

TOM: I won't be here.

JIM: How about your mother?

TOM: I'm like my father. The bastard son of a bastard! Did you notice how he's grinning in his picture in there? And he's been absent going on sixteen years!

JIM: You're just talking, you drip. How does your mother feel about it?

TOM: Shhh! Here comes Mother! Mother is not acquainted with my plans!

AMANDA *[coming through the portieres]*: Where are you all?

TOM: On the terrace, Mother.

[They start inside. She advances to them. Tom is distinctly shocked at her appearance. Even Jim blinks a little. He is making his first contact with girlish Southern vivacity and in spite of the night-school course in public speaking is somewhat thrown off the beam by the unexpected outlay of social charm. Certain responses are attempted by him but are swept aside by Amanda's gay laughter and

chatter. Tom is embarrassed but after the first shock Jim reacts very warmly. He grins and chuckles, is altogether won over. Image on screen: Amanda as a girl.]

AMANDA [*coyly smiling, shaking her girlish ringlets*]: Well, well, well, so this is Mr. O'Connor. Introductions entirely unnecessary. I've heard so much about you from my boy. I finally said to him, Tom—good gracious!—why don't you bring this paragon to supper? I'd like to meet this nice young man at the warehouse!—instead of just hearing him sing your praises so much! I don't know why my son is so stand-offish—that's not Southern behavior!

Let's sit down and—I think we could stand a little more air in here! Tom, leave the door open. I felt a nice fresh breeze a moment ago. Where has it gone to? Mmm, so warm already! And not quite summer, even. We're going to burn up when summer really gets started. However, we're having—we're having a very light supper. I think light things are better fo' this time of year. The same as light clothes are. Light clothes an' light food are what warm weather calls fo'. You know our blood gets so thick during th' winter—it takes a while fo' us to *adjust* ou'selves!—when the season changes . . . It's come so quick this year. I wasn't prepared. All of a sudden—heavens! Already summer! I ran to the trunk an' pulled out this light dress—terribly old! Historical almost! But feels so good—so good an' co-ol, y' know. . . .

TOM: Mother—

AMANDA: Yes, honey?

TOM: How about—supper?

AMANDA: Honey, you go ask Sister if supper is ready! You know that Sister is in full charge of supper! Tell her you hungry boys are waiting for it. [*To Jim.*] Have you met Laura?

JIM: She—

AMANDA: Let you in? Oh, good, you've met already! It's rare for a girl as sweet an' pretty as Laura to be domestic! But Laura is, thank heavens, not only pretty but also very domestic. I'm not at all. I never was a bit. I never could make a thing but angel-food cake. Well, in the South we had so many servants. Gone, gone, gone. All vestige of gracious living! Gone completely! I wasn't prepared for what the future brought me. All of my gentlemen callers were sons of planters and so of course I assumed that I would be married to one and raise my family on a large piece of land with plenty of servants. But man proposes—and woman accepts the proposal! To vary that old, old saying a little bit—I married no planter! I married a man who worked for the telephone company! That gallantly smiling gentleman over there! [*She points to the picture.*] A telephone man who—fell in love with long-distance! Now he travels and I don't even know where! But what am I going on for about my—tribulations? Tell me yours—I hope you don't have any! Tom?

TOM [*returning*]: Yes, Mother?

AMANDA: Is supper nearly ready?

TOM: It looks to me like supper is on the table.

AMANDA: Let me look— [*She rises prettily and looks through the portieres.*] Oh, lovely! But where is Sister?

TOM: Laura is not feeling well and she says that she thinks she'd better not come to the table.

AMANDA: What? Nonsense! Laura? Oh, Laura!

LAURA [*from the kitchenette, faintly*]: Yes, Mother.

AMANDA: You really must come to the table. We won't be seated until you come to the table! Come in, Mr. O'Connor. You sit over there, and I'll . . . Laura? Laura Wingfield! You're keeping us waiting, honey! We can't say grace until you come to the table!

[*The kitchenette door is pushed weakly open and Laura comes in. She is obviously quite faint, her lips trembling, her eyes wide and staring. She moves unsteadily toward the table. Screen legend: "Terror!" Outside a summer storm is coming on abruptly. The white curtains billow inward at the windows and there is a sorrowful murmur from the deep blue dusk. Laura suddenly stumbles; she catches at a chair with a faint moan.*]

TOM: Laura!

AMANDA: Laura!

[*There is a clap of thunder. Screen legend: "Ah!"*]

[*Despairingly.*] Why, Laura, you *are* ill, darling! Tom, help your sister into the living room, dear! Sit in the living room, Laura—rest on the sofa. Well! [*To Jim as Tom helps his sister to the sofa in the living room.*] Standing over the hot stove made her ill! I told her that it was just too warm this evening, but—

[*Tom comes back to the table.*]

Is Laura all right now?

TOM: Yes.

AMANDA: What *is* that? Rain? A nice cool rain has come up! [*She gives Jim a frightened look.*] I think we may—have grace—now ...

[*Tom looks at her stupidly.*] Tom, honey—you say grace!

TOM: Oh ... "For these and all thy mercies—"

[*They bow their heads, Amanda stealing a nervous glance at Jim. In the living room Laura, stretched on the sofa, clenches her hand to her lips, to hold back a shuddering sob.*]

God's Holy Name be praised—

[*The scene dims out.*] great time

69

SCENE SEVEN

It is half an hour later. Dinner is just being finished in the dining room, Laura is still huddled upon the sofa, her feet drawn under her, her head resting on a pale blue pillow, her eyes wide and mysteriously watchful. The new floor lamp with its shade of rose-colored silk gives a soft, becoming light to her face, bringing out the fragile, unearthly prettiness which usually escapes attention. From outside there is a steady murmur of rain, but it is slackening and soon stops; the air outside becomes pale and luminous as the moon breaks through the clouds. A moment after the curtain rises, the lights in both rooms flicker and go out.

JIM: Hey, there, Mr. Light Bulb!

[Amanda laughs nervously. Legend on screen: "Suspension of a public service."]

AMANDA: Where was Moses when the lights went out? Ha-ha. Do you know the answer to that one, Mr. O'Connor?

JIM: No, Ma'am, what's the answer?

AMANDA: In the dark!

[Jim laughs appreciatively.]

Everybody sit still. I'll light the candles. Isn't it lucky we have them on the table? Where's a match? Which of you gentlemen can provide a match?

JIM: Here.

AMANDA: Thank you, Sir.

JIM: Not at all, Ma'am!

AMANDA *[as she lights the candles]*: I guess the fuse has burnt out.

Mr. O'Connor, can you tell a burnt-out fuse? I know I can't and Tom is a total loss when it comes to mechanics.

[They rise from the table and go into the kitchenette, from where their voices are heard.]

Oh, be careful you don't bump into something. We don't want our gentleman caller to break his neck. Now wouldn't that be a fine howdy-do?

JIM: Ha-ha! Where is the fuse-box?

AMANDA: Right here next to the stove. Can you see anything?

JIM: Just a minute.

AMANDA: Isn't electricity a mysterious thing? Wasn't it Benjamin Franklin who tied a key to a kite? We live in such a mysterious universe, don't we? Some people say that science clears up all the mysteries for us. In my opinion it only creates more! Have you found it yet?

JIM: No, Ma'am. All these fuses look okay to me.

AMANDA: Tom!

TOM: Yes, Mother?

AMANDA: That light bill I gave you several days ago. The one I told you we got the notices about?

[Legend on screen: "Ha!"]

TOM: Oh—yeah.

AMANDA: You didn't neglect to pay it by any chance?

TOM: Why, I—

AMANDA: Didn't! I might have known it!

JIM: Shakespeare probably wrote a poem on that light bill, Mrs. Wingfield.

AMANDA: I might have known better than to trust him with it! There's such a high price for negligence in this world!

JIM: Maybe the poem will win a ten-dollar prize.

AMANDA: We'll just have to spend the remainder of the evening in the nineteenth century, before Mr. Edison made the Mazda lamp!

JIM: Candlelight is my favorite kind of light.

AMANDA: That shows you're romantic! But that's no excuse for Tom. Well, we got through dinner. Very considerate of them to let us get through dinner before they plunged us into everlasting darkness, wasn't it, Mr. O'Connor?

JIM: Ha-ha!

AMANDA: Tom, as a penalty for your carelessness you can help me with the dishes.

JIM: Let me give you a hand.

AMANDA: Indeed you will not!

JIM: I ought to be good for something.

AMANDA: Good for something? [*Her tone is rhapsodic.*] *You?* Why, Mr. O'Connor, nobody, *nobody's* given me this much entertainment in years—as you have!

JIM: Aw, now, Mrs. Wingfield!

AMANDA: I'm not exaggerating, not one bit! But Sister is all by her lonesome. You go keep her company in the parlor! I'll give you this lovely old candelabrum that used to be on the altar at the Church of the Heavenly Rest. It was melted a little out of shape when the church burnt down. Lightning struck it one spring. Gypsy Jones was holding a revival at the time and he intimated that the church was destroyed because the Episcopalians gave card parties.

JIM: Ha-ha.

AMANDA: And how about you coaxing Sister to drink a little wine? I think it would be good for her! Can you carry both at once?

JIM: Sure. I'm Superman!

AMANDA: Now, Thomas, get into this apron!

[*Jim comes into the dining room, carrying the candelabrum, its candles lighted, in one hand and a glass of wine in the other. The door of the kitchenette swings closed on Amanda's gay laughter; the flickering light approaches the portieres. Laura sits up nervously as Jim enters. She can hardly speak from the almost intolerable strain of being alone with a stranger.*

Screen legend: "I don't suppose you remember me at all!"

At first, before Jim's warmth overcomes her paralyzing shyness, Laura's voice is thin and breathless, as though she had just run up a steep flight of stairs. Jim's attitude is gently humorous. While the incident is apparently unimportant, it is to Laura the climax of her secret life.]

JIM: Hello there, Laura.

LAURA [*faintly*]: Hello. [*She clears her throat.*]

JIM: How are you feeling now? Better?

LAURA: Yes. Yes, thank you.

JIM: This is for you. A little dandelion wine. [*He extends the glass toward her with extravagant gallantry.*]

LAURA: Thank you.

JIM: Drink it—but don't get drunk! [*He laughs heartily. Laura takes the glass uncertainly; she laughs shyly.*] Where shall I set the candles?

LAURA: Oh—oh, anywhere . . .

JIM: How about here on the floor? Any objections?

LAURA: No.

JIM: I'll spread a newspaper under to catch the drippings. I like to sit on the floor. Mind if I do?

LAURA: Oh, no.

JIM: Give me a pillow?

LAURA: What?

JIM: A pillow!

LAURA: Oh . . . [*She hands him one quickly.*]

JIM: How about you? Don't you like to sit on the floor?

LAURA: Oh—yes.

JIM: Why don't you, then?

LAURA: I—will.

JIM: Take a pillow!

[*Laura does. She sits on the floor on the other side of the candelabrum. Jim crosses his legs and smiles engagingly at her.*]

I can't hardly see you sitting way over there.

LAURA: I can—see you.

JIM: I know, but that's not fair, I'm in the limelight.

[*Laura moves her pillow closer.*]

Good! Now I can see you! Comfortable?

LAURA: Yes.

JIM: So am I. Comfortable as a cow! Will you have some gum?

LAURA: No, thank you.

JIM: I think that I will indulge, with your permission. [*He musingly unwraps a stick of gum and holds it up.*] Think of the fortune made by the guy that invented the first piece of chewing gum. Amazing, huh? The Wrigley Building is one of the sights of Chicago—I saw it when I went up to the Century of Progress. Did you take in the Century of Progress?

LAURA: No, I didn't.

JIM: Well, it was quite a wonderful exposition. What impressed me most was the Hall of Science. Gives you an idea of what the future will be in America, even more wonderful than the present time is! [*There is a pause. Jim smiles at her.*] Your brother tells me you're shy. Is that right, Laura?

LAURA: I—don't know.

JIM: I judge you to be an old-fashioned type of girl. Well, I think that's a pretty good type to be. Hope you don't think I'm being too personal—do you?

LAURA: [*hastily, out of embarrassment*]: I believe I *will* take a piece of gum, if you—don't mind. [*Clearing her throat.*] Mr. O'Connor, have you—kept up with your singing?

JIM: Singing? Me?

LAURA: Yes. I remember what a beautiful voice you had.

JIM: When did you hear me sing?

[*Laura does not answer, and in the long pause which follows a man's voice is heard singing offstage.*]

VOICE:
O blow, ye winds, heigh-ho,
A-roving I will go!
   I'm off to my love
   With a boxing glove—
Ten thousand miles away!

JIM: You say you've heard me sing?

LAURA: Oh, yes! Yes, very often . . . I—don't suppose—you remember me—at all?

JIM [*smiling doubtfully*]: You know I have an idea I've seen you before. I had that idea soon as you opened the door. It seemed almost like I was about to remember your name. But the name that I started to call you—wasn't a name! And so I stopped myself before I said it.

LAURA: Wasn't it—Blue Roses?

JIM [*springing up, grinning*]: Blue Roses! My gosh, yes—Blue Roses! That's what I had on my tongue when you opened the door! Isn't it funny what tricks your memory plays? I didn't connect you with high school somehow or other. But that's where it was; it was high school. I didn't even know you were Shakespeare's sister! Gosh, I'm sorry.

LAURA: I didn't expect you to. You—barely knew me!

JIM: But we did have a speaking acquaintance, huh?

LAURA: Yes, we—spoke to each other.

JIM: When did you recognize me?

LAURA: Oh, right away!

JIM: Soon as I came in the door?

LAURA: When I heard your name I thought it was probably you. I knew that Tom used to know you a little in high school. So when you came in the door—well, then I was—sure.

JIM: Why didn't you *say* something, then?

LAURA [*breathlessly*]: I didn't know what to say, I was—too surprised! Getting more comfortable

JIM: For goodness' sakes! You know, this sure is funny!

LAURA: Yes! Yes, isn't it, though . . .

JIM: Didn't we have a class in something together?

LAURA: Yes, we did.

JIM: What class was that?

LAURA: It was—singing—chorus!

JIM: Aw!

LAURA: I sat across the aisle from you in the auditorium.

JIM: Aw.

LAURA: Mondays, Wednesdays, and Fridays. sus

JIM: Now I remember—you always came in late.

LAURA: Yes, it was so hard for me, getting upstairs. I had that brace on my leg—it clumped so loud!

JIM: I never heard any clumping.

LAURA [*wincing at the recollection*]: To me it sounded like—thunder!

JIM: Well, well, well, I never even noticed.

LAURA: And everybody was seated before I came in. I had to walk in front of all those people. My seat was in the back row. I had to go clumping all the way up the aisle with everyone watching!

JIM: You shouldn't have been self-conscious.

LAURA: I know, but I was. It was always such a relief when the singing started.

JIM: Aw, yes, I've placed you now! I used to call you Blue Roses. How was it that I got started calling you that?

LAURA: I was out of school a little while with pleurosis. When I came back you asked me what was the matter. I said I had pleurosis—you thought I said *Blue Roses*. That's what you always called me after that!

JIM: I hope you didn't mind.

LAURA: Oh, no—I liked it. You see, I wasn't acquainted with many—people. . . .

JIM: As I remember you sort of stuck by yourself.

LAURA: I—I—never have had much luck at—making friends.

JIM: I don't see why you wouldn't.

LAURA: Well, I—started out badly.

JIM: You mean being—

LAURA: Yes, it sort of—stood between me—

JIM: You shouldn't have let it!

LAURA: I know, but it did, and—

JIM: You were shy with people!

LAURA: I tried not to be but never could—

JIM: Overcome it?

LAURA: No, I—I never could!

JIM: I guess being shy is something you have to work out of kind of gradually.

LAURA [*sorrowfully*]: Yes—I guess it—   Chemistry

JIM: Takes time!

LAURA: Yes—

JIM: People are not so dreadful when you know them. That's what you have to remember! And everybody has problems, not just you, but practically everybody has got some problems. You think of yourself as having the only problems, as being the only one who is disappointed. But just look around you and you will see lots of people as disappointed as you are. For instance, I hoped when I was going to high school that I would be further along at this time, six years later, than I am now. You remember that wonderful write-up I had in *The Torch*?

LAURA: Yes! [*She rises and crosses to the table.*]

JIM: It said I was bound to succeed in anything I went into!

[*Laura returns with the high school yearbook.*]

Holy Jeez! *The Torch!*

[*He accepts it reverently. They smile across the book with mutual wonder. Laura crouches beside him and they begin to turn the pages. Laura's shyness is dissolving in his warmth.*]

LAURA: Here you are in *The Pirates of Penzance!*

JIM [*wistfully*]: I sang the baritone lead in that operetta.

LAURA [*raptly*]: So—*beautifully!*

JIM [*protesting*]: Aw—

LAURA: Yes, yes—beautifully—beautifully!

JIM: You heard me?

LAURA: All three times!

JIM: No!

LAURA: Yes!

JIM: All three performances?

LAURA [*looking down*]: Yes.

JIM: Why?

LAURA: I—wanted to ask you to—autograph my program. [*She takes the program from the back of the yearbook and shows it to him.*]

JIM: Why didn't you ask me to?

LAURA: You were always surrounded by your own friends so much that I never had a chance to.

JIM: You should have just—

LAURA: Well, I—thought you might think I was—

JIM: Thought I might think you was—what?

LAURA: Oh—

JIM [*with reflective relish*]: I was beleaguered by females in those days.

LAURA: You were terribly popular!

JIM: Yeah—

LAURA: You had such a—friendly way—

JIM: I was spoiled in high school.

LAURA: Everybody—liked you!

JIM: Including you?

LAURA: I—yes, I—did, too— [*She gently closes the book in her lap.*]

JIM: Well, well, well! Give me that program, Laura. [*She hands it to him. He signs it with a flourish.*] There you are—better late than never!

LAURA: Oh, I—what a—surprise!

JIM: My signature isn't worth very much right now. But some day—maybe—it will increase in value! Being disappointed is one thing and being discouraged is something else. I am disappointed but I am not discouraged. I'm twenty-three years old. How old are you?

LAURA: I'll be twenty-four in June.

JIM: That's not old age!

LAURA: No, but—

JIM: You finished high school?

LAURA [*with difficulty*]: I didn't go back.

JIM: You mean you dropped out?

LAURA: I made bad grades in my final examinations. [*She rises and replaces the book and the program on the table. Her voice is strained.*] How is—Emily Meisenbach getting along?

JIM: Oh, that kraut-head!

LAURA: Why do you call her that?

JIM: That's what she was.

LAURA: You're not still—going with her?

JIM: I never see her.

LAURA: It said in the "Personal" section that you were—engaged!

JIM: I know, but I wasn't impressed by that—propaganda!

LAURA: It wasn't—the truth?

JIM: Only in Emily's optimistic opinion!

LAURA: Oh—

[Legend: "What have you done since high school?"
    Jim lights a cigarette and leans indolently back on his elbows smiling at Laura with a warmth and charm which lights her inwardly with altar candles. She remains by the table, picks up a piece from the glass menagerie collection, and turns it in her hands to cover her tumult.]

JIM [after several reflective puffs on his cigarette]: What have you done since high school?

[She seems not to hear him.]

Huh?

[Laura looks up.]

I said what have you done since high school, Laura?

LAURA: Nothing much.

JIM: You must have been doing something these six long years.

LAURA: Yes.

JIM: Well, then, such as what?

LAURA: I took a business course at business college—

JIM: How did that work out?

LAURA: Well, not very—well—I had to drop out, it gave me—indigestion—

[Jim laughs gently.]

JIM: What are you doing now?

LAURA: I don't do anything—much. Oh, please don't think I sit around doing nothing! My glass collection takes up a good deal of time. Glass is something you have to take good care of.

JIM: What did you say—about glass?

LAURA: Collection I said—I have one— [*She clears her throat and turns away again, acutely shy.*] *psychoanalyze*

JIM [*abruptly*]: You know what I judge to be the trouble with you? Inferiority complex! Know what that is? That's what they call it when someone low-rates himself! I understand it because I had it, too. Although my case was not so aggravated as yours seems to be. I had it until I took up public speaking, developed my voice, and learned that I had an aptitude for science. Before that time I never thought of myself as being outstanding in any way whatsoever! Now I've never made a regular study of it, but I have a friend who says I can analyze people better than doctors that make a profession of it. I don't claim that to be necessarily true, but I can sure guess a person's psychology, Laura! [*He takes out his gum.*] Excuse me, Laura. I always take it out when the flavor is gone. I'll use this scrap of paper to wrap it in. I know how it is to get it stuck on a shoe. [*He wraps the gum in paper and puts it in his pocket.*] Yep—that's what I judge to be your principal trouble. A lack of confidence in yourself as a person. You don't have the proper amount of faith in yourself. I'm basing that fact on a number of your remarks and also on certain observations I've made. For instance that clumping you thought was so awful in high school. You say that you even dreaded to walk into class. You see what you did? You dropped out of school, you gave up an education because of a clump, which as far as I know was practically non-existent! A little physical defect is what you have. Hardly noticeable even! Magnified thousands of times by imagination! You know what my strong advice to you is? Think of yourself as *superior* in some way!

LAURA: In what way would I think?

JIM: Why, man alive, Laura! Just look about you a little. What do you see? A world full of common people! All of 'em born and all of 'em going to die! Which of them has one-tenth of your good points! Or mine! Or anyone else's, as far as that goes—gosh! Everybody excels in some one thing. Some in many! [*He unconsciously glances at himself in the mirror.*] All you've got to do is discover in *what!* Take me, for instance. [*He adjusts his tie at the mirror.*] My interest happens to lie in electro-dynamics. I'm taking a course in radio engineering at night school, Laura, on top of a fairly responsible job at the warehouse. I'm taking that course and studying public speaking.

LAURA: Ohhhh. *dreams*

JIM: Because I believe in the future of television! [*Turning his back to her.*] I wish to be ready to go up right along with it. Therefore I'm planning to get in on the ground floor. In fact I've already made the right connections and all that remains is for the industry itself to get under way! Full steam— [*His eyes are starry.*] *Knowledge*—Zzzzzp! *Money*—Zzzzzp!—*Power!* That's the cycle democracy is built on! [*His attitude is convincingly dynamic. Laura stares at him, even her shyness eclipsed in her absolute wonder. He suddenly grins.*] I guess you think I think a lot of myself!

LAURA: No—o-o-o, I—

JIM: Now how about you? Isn't there something you take more interest in than anything else?

LAURA: Well, I do—as I said—have my—glass collection—

[*A peal of girlish laughter rings from the kitchenette.*]

JIM: I'm not right sure I know what you're talking about. What kind of glass is it?

LAURA: Little articles of it, they're ornaments mostly! Most of them are little animals made out of glass, the tiniest little animals in the world. Mother calls them a glass menagerie! Here's an example of one, if you'd like to see it! This one is one of the oldest. It's nearly thirteen.

[*Music: "The Glass Menagerie." He stretches out his hand.*]

Oh, be careful—if you breathe, it breaks!

JIM: I'd better not take it. I'm pretty clumsy with things.

LAURA: Go on, I trust you with him! [*She places the piece in his palm.*] There now—you're holding him gently! Hold him over the light, he loves the light! You see how the light shines through him?

JIM: It sure does shine!

LAURA: I shouldn't be partial, but he is my favorite one.

JIM: What kind of a thing is this one supposed to be?

LAURA: Haven't you noticed the single horn on his forehead?

JIM: A unicorn, huh?

LAURA: Mmmm-hmmm!

JIM: Unicorns—aren't they extinct in the modern world?

LAURA: I know!

JIM: Poor little fellow, he must feel sort of lonesome.

LAURA [*smiling*]: Well, if he does, he doesn't complain about it. He stays on a shelf with some horses that don't have horns and all of them seem to get along nicely together.

JIM: How do you know?

LAURA [*lightly*]: I haven't heard any arguments among them!

JIM [*grinning*]: No arguments, huh? Well, that's a pretty good sign! Where shall I set him?

LAURA: Put him on the table. They all like a change of scenery once in a while! ~her only friends

JIM: Well, well, well, well— [*He places the glass piece on the table, then raises his arms and stretches.*] Look how big my shadow is when I stretch!

LAURA: Oh, oh, yes—it stretches across the ceiling!

JIM [*crossing to the door*]: I think it's stopped raining. [*He opens the fire-escape door and the background music changes to a dance tune.*] Where does the music come from?

LAURA: From the Paradise Dance Hall across the alley.

JIM: How about cutting the rug a little, Miss Wingfield?

LAURA: Oh, I—

JIM: Or is your program filled up? Let me have a look at it. [*He grasps an imaginary card.*] Why, every dance is taken! I'll just have to scratch some out.

[*Waltz music: "La Golondrina."*]

Ahhh, a waltz! [*He executes some sweeping turns by himself, then holds his arms toward Laura.*]

LAURA [*breathlessly*]: I—can't dance!

JIM: There you go, that inferiority stuff!

LAURA: I've never danced in my life!

JIM: Come on, try!

LAURA: Oh, but I'd step on you!

JIM: I'm not made out of glass.

LAURA: How—how—how do we start?

JIM: Just leave it to me. You hold your arms out a little.

LAURA: Like this?

JIM [*taking her in his arms*]: A little bit higher. Right. Now don't tighten up, that's the main thing about it—relax.

LAURA [*laughing breathlessly*]: It's hard not to.

JIM: Okay.

LAURA: I'm afraid you can't budge me.

JIM: What do you bet I can't? [*He swings her into motion.*]

LAURA: Goodness, yes, you can!

JIM: Let yourself go, now, Laura, just let yourself go.

LAURA: I'm—

JIM: Come on!

LAURA: —trying!

JIM: Not so stiff—easy does it!

LAURA: I know but I'm—

JIM: Loosen th' backbone! There now, that's a lot better.

LAURA: Am I?

JIM: Lots, lots better! [*He moves her about the room in a clumsy waltz.*]

LAURA: Oh, my!

JIM: Ha-ha!

LAURA: Oh, my goodness!

JIM: Ha-ha-ha!

[*They suddenly bump into the table, and the glass piece on it falls to the floor. Jim stops the dance.*]

What did we hit on?

LAURA: Table.

JIM: Did something fall off it? I think—

LAURA: Yes.

JIM: I hope that it wasn't the little glass horse with the horn!

LAURA: Yes. [*She stoops to pick it up.*]

JIM: Aw, aw, aw. Is it broken?

LAURA: Now it is just like all the other horses.

JIM: It's lost its—

LAURA: Horn! It doesn't matter. Maybe it's a blessing in disguise.

↳ new reactions

JIM: You'll never forgive me. I bet that that was your favorite piece of glass.

LAURA: I don't have favorites much. It's no tragedy, Freckles. Glass breaks so easily. No matter how careful you are. The traffic jars the shelves and things fall off them.

JIM: Still I'm awfully sorry that I was the cause.

LAURA [*smiling*]: I'll just imagine he had an operation. The horn was removed to make him feel less—freakish! [*They both laugh.*] Now he will feel more at home with the other horses, the ones that don't have horns. . . .

JIM: Ha-ha, that's very funny! [*Suddenly he is serious.*] I'm glad to see that you have a sense of humor. You know—you're—well—very different! Surprisingly different from anyone else I know! [*His voice becomes soft and hesitant with a genuine feeling.*] Do you mind me telling you that?

[*Laura is abashed beyond speech.*]

I mean it in a nice way—

[*Laura nods shyly, looking away.*]

JIM: You make me feel sort of—I don't know how to put it! I'm usually pretty good at expressing things, but—this is something that I don't know how to say!

[*Laura touches her throat and clears it—turns the broken unicorn in her hands. His voice becomes softer.*]

Has anyone ever told you that you were pretty?

[*There is a pause, and the music rises slightly. Laura looks up slowly, with wonder, and shakes her head.*]

Well, you are! In a very different way from anyone else. And all the nicer because of the difference, too.

[His voice becomes low and husky. Laura turns away, nearly faint with the novelty of her emotions.]

I wish that you were my sister. I'd teach you to have some confidence in yourself. The different people are not like other people, but being different is nothing to be ashamed of. Because other people are not such wonderful people. They're one hundred times one thousand. You're one times one! They walk all over the earth. You just stay here. They're common as—weeds, but—you—well, you're—*Blue Roses!*

[Image on screen: Blue Roses. The music changes.]

LAURA: But blue is wrong for—roses. . . .

JIM: It's right for you! You're—pretty!

LAURA: In what respect am I pretty?

JIM: In all respects—believe me! Your eyes—your hair—are pretty! Your hands are pretty! [*He catches hold of her hand.*] You think I'm making this up because I'm invited to dinner and have to be nice. Oh, I could do that! I could put on an act for you, Laura, and say lots of things without being very sincere. But this time I am. I'm talking to you sincerely. I happened to notice you had this inferiority complex that keeps you from feeling comfortable with people. Somebody needs to build your confidence up and make you proud instead of shy and turning away and—blushing. Somebody—ought to—*kiss you, Laura!*

[His hand slips slowly up her arm to her shoulder as the music swells tumultuously. He suddenly turns her about and kisses her on the lips. When he releases her, Laura sinks on the sofa with a bright, dazed look. Jim backs away and fishes in his pocket for a cigarette. Legend on screen: "A souvenir."]

Stumblejohn!

[He lights the cigarette, avoiding her look. There is a peal of girlish laughter from Amanda in the kitchenette. Laura slowly raises and opens her hand. It still contains the little broken glass animal. She looks at it with a tender, bewildered expression.]

Stumblejohn! I shouldn't have done that—that was way off the beam. You don't smoke, do you?

[*She looks up, smiling, not hearing the question. He sits beside her rather gingerly. She looks at him speechlessly—waiting. He coughs decorously and moves a little farther aside as he considers the situation and senses her feelings, dimly, with perturbation. He speaks gently.*]

Would you—care for a mint?

[*She doesn't seem to hear him but her look grows brighter even.*]

Peppermint? Life Saver? My pocket's a regular drugstore—wherever I go. . . . [*He pops a mint in his mouth. Then he gulps and decides to make a clean breast of it. He speaks slowly and gingerly.*] Laura, you know, if I had a sister like you, I'd do the same thing as Tom. I'd bring out fellows and—introduce her to them. The right type of boys—of a type to—appreciate her. Only—well—he made a mistake about me. Maybe I've got no call to be saying this. That may not have been the idea in having me over. But what if it was? There's nothing wrong about that. The only trouble is that in my case—I'm not in a situation to—do the right thing. I can't take down your number and say I'll phone. I can't call up next week and—ask for a date. I thought I had better explain the situation in case you—misunderstood it and—I hurt your feelings. . . .

[*There is a pause. Slowly, very slowly, Laura's look changes, her eyes returning slowly from his to the glass figure in her palm. Amanda utters another gay laugh in the kitchenette.*]

LAURA [*faintly*]: You—won't—call again?

JIM: No, Laura, I can't. [*He rises from the sofa.*] As I was just explaining, I've—got strings on me. Laura, I've—been going steady! I go out all the time with a girl named Betty. She's a home-girl like you, and Catholic, and Irish, and in a great many ways we—get along fine. I met her last summer on a moonlight boat trip up the river to Alton, on the *Majestic*. Well—right away from the start it was—love!

[Legend: "Love!" Laura sways slightly forward and grips the arm of the sofa. He fails to notice, now enrapt in his own comfortable being.]

Being in love has made a new man of me!

[Leaning stiffly forward, clutching the arm of the sofa, Laura struggles visibly with her storm. But Jim is oblivious; she is a long way off.]

The power of love is really pretty tremendous! Love is something that—changes the whole world, Laura!

[The storm abates a little and Laura leans back. He notices her again.]

It happened that Betty's aunt took sick, she got a wire and had to go to Centralia. So Tom—when he asked me to dinner—I naturally just accepted the invitation, not knowing that you—that he—that I— *[He stops awkwardly.]* Huh—I'm a stumblejohn!

[He flops back on the sofa. The holy candles on the altar of Laura's face have been snuffed out. There is a look of almost infinite desolation. Jim glances at her uneasily.]

I wish that you would—say something.

[She bites her lip which was trembling and then bravely smiles. She opens her hand again on the broken glass figure. Then she gently takes his hand and raises it level with her own. She carefully places the unicorn in the palm of his hand, then pushes his fingers closed upon it.]

What are you—doing that for? You want me to have him? Laura?

[She nods.]

What for?

LAURA: A—souvenir. . . .

[She rises unsteadily and crouches beside the Victrola to wind it up. Legend on screen: "Things have a way of turning out so badly!" Or image: Gentleman caller waving goodbye—gaily.

At this moment Amanda rushes brightly back into the living room. She bears a pitcher of fruit punch in an old-fashioned cut-glass pitcher, and a plate of macaroons. The plate has a gold border and poppies painted on it.]

AMANDA: Well, well, well! Isn't the air delightful after the shower? I've made you children a little liquid refreshment. [*She turns gaily to Jim.*] Jim, do you know that song about lemonade?

> "Lemonade, lemonade
> Made in the shade and stirred with a spade—
> Good enough for any old maid!"

JIM [*uneasily*]: Ha-ha! No—I never heard it.

AMANDA: Why, Laura! You look so serious!

JIM: We were having a serious conversation.

AMANDA: Good! Now you're better acquainted!

JIM [*uncertainly*]: Ha-ha! Yes.

AMANDA: You modern young people are much more serious-minded than my generation. I was so gay as a girl!

JIM: You haven't changed, Mrs. Wingfield.

AMANDA: Tonight I'm rejuvenated! The gaiety of the occasion, Mr. O'Connor! [*She tosses her head with a peal of laughter, spilling some lemonade.*] Oooo! I'm baptizing myself!

JIM: Here—let me—

AMANDA [*setting the pitcher down*]: There now. I discovered we had some maraschino cherries. I dumped them in, juice and all!

JIM: You shouldn't have gone to that trouble, Mrs. Wingfield.

AMANDA: Trouble, trouble? Why, it was loads of fun! Didn't you hear me cutting up in the kitchen? I bet your ears were burning! I told Tom how outdone with him I was for keeping you to himself so long a time! He should have brought you over much, much sooner! Well, now that you've found your way, I want you to be a very frequent caller! Not just occasional but all the time. Oh, we're going to have a lot of gay times together! I see them coming! Mmm, just breathe that air! So fresh, and the moon's so pretty! I'll skip back out—I know where my place is when young folks are having a—serious conversation!

JIM: Oh, don't go out, Mrs. Wingfield. The fact of the matter is I've got to be going.

AMANDA: Going, now? You're joking! Why, it's only the shank of the evening, Mr. O'Connor!

JIM: Well, you know how it is.

AMANDA: You mean you're a young workingman and have to keep workingmen's hours. We'll let you off early tonight. But only on the condition that next time you stay later. What's the best night for you? Isn't Saturday night the best night for you workingmen?

JIM: I have a couple of time-clocks to punch, Mrs. Wingfield. One at morning, another one at night!

AMANDA: My, but you *are* ambitious! You work at night, too?

JIM: No, Ma'am, not work but—Betty!

[*He crosses deliberately to pick up his hat. The band at the Paradise Dance Hall goes into a tender waltz.*]

AMANDA: Betty? Betty? Who's—Betty!

[*There is an ominous cracking sound in the sky.*]

JIM: Oh, just a girl. The girl I go steady with!

[*He smiles charmingly. The sky falls. Legend: "The Sky Falls."*]

AMANDA [*a long-drawn exhalation*]: Ohhhh . . . Is it a serious romance, Mr. O'Connor?

JIM: We're going to be married the second Sunday in June.

AMANDA: Ohhhh—how nice! Tom didn't mention that you were engaged to be married.

JIM: The cat's not out of the bag at the warehouse yet. You know how they are. They call you Romeo and stuff like that. [*He stops at the oval mirror to put on his hat. He carefully shapes the brim and the crown to give a discreetly dashing effect.*] It's been a wonderful evening, Mrs. Wingfield. I guess this is what they mean by Southern hospitality.

AMANDA: It really wasn't anything at all.

JIM: I hope it don't seem like I'm rushing off. But I promised Betty I'd pick her up at the Wabash depot, an' by the time I get my jalopy down there her train'll be in. Some women are pretty upset if you keep 'em waiting.

AMANDA: Yes, I know—the tyranny of women! [*She extends her hand.*] Goodbye, Mr. O'Connor. I wish you luck—and happiness—and success! All three of them, and so does Laura! Don't you, Laura?

LAURA: Yes!

JIM [*taking Laura's hand*]: Goodbye, Laura. I'm certainly going to treasure that souvenir. And don't you forget the good advice I gave you. [*He raises his voice to a cheery shout.*] So long, Shakespeare! Thanks again, ladies. Good night!

[*He grins and ducks jauntily out. Still bravely grimacing, Amanda closes the door on the gentleman caller. Then she turns back to the room with a puzzled expression. She and Laura don't dare to face each other. Laura crouches beside the Victrola to wind it.*]

AMANDA [*faintly*]: Things have a way of turning out so badly. I don't believe that I would play the Victrola. Well, well—well! Our gentleman caller was engaged to be married! [*She raises her voice.*] Tom!

TOM [*from the kitchenette*]: Yes, Mother?

AMANDA: Come in here a minute. I want to tell you something awfully funny.

TOM [*entering with a macaroon and a glass of the lemonade*]: Has the gentleman caller gotten away already?

AMANDA: The gentleman caller has made an early departure. What a wonderful joke you played on us!

TOM: How do you mean?

AMANDA: You didn't mention that he was engaged to be married.

TOM: Jim? Engaged?

AMANDA: That's what he just informed us.

TOM: I'll be jiggered! I didn't know about that.

AMANDA: That seems very peculiar.

TOM: What's peculiar about it?

AMANDA: Didn't you call him your best friend down at the warehouse?

TOM: He is, but how did I know?

AMANDA: It seems extremely peculiar that you wouldn't know your best friend was going to be married!

TOM: The warehouse is where I work, not where I know things about people!

AMANDA: You don't know things anywhere! You live in a dream; you manufacture illusions!

[He crosses to the door.]

Where are you going?

TOM: I'm going to the movies.

AMANDA: That's right, now that you've had us make such fools of ourselves. The effort, the preparations, all the expense! The new floor lamp, the rug, the clothes for Laura! All for what? To entertain some other girl's fiancé! Go to the movies, go! Don't think about us, a mother deserted, an unmarried sister who's crippled and has no job! Don't let anything interfere with your selfish pleasure! Just go, go, go—to the movies!

TOM: All right, I will! The more you shout about my selfishness to me the quicker I'll go, and I won't go to the movies!

AMANDA: Go, then! Go to the moon—you selfish dreamer!

[*Tom smashes his glass on the floor. He plunges out on the fire escape, slamming the door. Laura screams in fright. The dance-hall music becomes louder. Tom stands on the fire escape, gripping the rail. The moon breaks through the storm clouds, illuminating his face.*

Legend on screen: "And so goodbye . . ."

Tom's closing speech is timed with what is happening inside the house. We see, as though through soundproof glass, that Amanda appears to be making a comforting speech to Laura, who is huddled upon the sofa. Now that we cannot hear the mother's speech, her silliness is gone and she has dignity and tragic beauty. Laura's hair hides her face until, at the end of the speech, she lifts her head to smile at her mother. Amanda's gestures are slow and graceful, almost dancelike, as she comforts her daughter. At the end of her speech she glances a moment at the father's picture—then withdraws through the portieres. At the close of Tom's speech, Laura blows out the candles, ending the play.]

TOM: I didn't go to the moon, I went much further—for time is the longest distance between two places. Not long after that I was fired for writing a poem on the lid of a shoe-box. I left Saint Louis. I descended the steps of this fire escape for a last time and followed, from then on, in my father's footsteps, attempting to find in motion what was lost in space. I traveled around a great deal. The cities swept about me like dead leaves, leaves that were brightly colored but torn away from the branches. I would have stopped, but I was pursued by something. It always came upon me unawares, taking me altogether by surprise. Perhaps it was a familiar bit of music. Perhaps it was only a piece of transparent glass. Perhaps I am walking along a street at night, in some strange city, before I have found companions. I pass the lighted window of a shop where perfume is sold. The window is filled with pieces of colored glass, tiny transparent bottles in delicate colors, like bits of a shattered rainbow. Then all at once my sister touches my shoulder. I turn around and look into her eyes. Oh, Laura, Laura, I tried to leave you behind me, but I am more faithful than I intended to be! I reach for a cigarette, I cross the street, I run into the movies or a bar, I buy a drink, I speak to the nearest stranger—anything that can blow your candles out!

[Laura bends over the candles.]

For nowadays the world is lit by lightning! Blow out your candles, Laura—and so goodbye. . . .

[She blows the candles out.]

THE CATASTROPHE OF SUCCESS

This winter marked the third anniversary of the Chicago opening of *The Glass Menagerie*, an event which terminated one part of my life and began another about as different in all external circumstances as could well be imagined. I was snatched out of virtual oblivion and thrust into sudden prominence, and from the precarious tenancy of furnished rooms about the country I was removed to a suite in a first-class Manhattan hotel. My experience was not unique. Success has often come that abruptly into the lives of Americans. The Cinderella story is our favorite national myth, the cornerstone of the film industry if not of the Democracy itself. I have seen it enacted on the screen so often that I am now inclined to yawn at it, not with disbelief but with an attitude of Who Cares! Anyone with such beautiful teeth and hair as the screen protagonist of such a story was bound to have a good time one way or another, and you could bet your bottom dollar and all the tea in China that that one would not be caught dead or alive at any meeting involving a social conscience.

No, my experience was not exceptional, but neither was it quite ordinary, and if you are willing to accept the somewhat eclectic proposition that I had not been writing with such an experience in mind—and many people are not willing to believe that a playwright is interested in anything but popular success—there may be some point in comparing the two estates.

The sort of life which I had had previous to this popular success was one that required endurance, a life of clawing and scratching along a sheer surface and holding on tight with raw fingers to every inch of rock higher than the one caught hold of before, but it was a good life because it was the sort of life for which the human organism is created.

I was not aware of how much vital energy had gone into this struggle until the struggle was removed. I was out on a level plateau with my arm still thrashing and my lungs still grabbing at air that no longer resisted. This was security at last.

I sat down and looked about me and was suddenly very depressed. I thought to myself, this is just a period of adjustment. Tomorrow morning I will wake up in this first-class hotel suite above the discreet hum of an East Side boulevard and I will appreciate its elegance and luxuriate in its comforts and know that I have arrived at our American plan of Olympus. Tomorrow morning when I look at the green satin sofa I will fall in love with it. It is only temporarily that the green satin looks like slime on stagnant water.

But in the morning the inoffensive little sofa looked more revolting than the night before, and I was already getting too fat for the $125 suit which a fashionable acquaintance had selected for me. In the suite things began to break accidentally. An arm came off the sofa. Cigarette burns appeared on the polished surface of the furniture. Windows were left open and a rainstorm flooded the suite. But the maid always put it straight and the patience of the management was inexhaustible. Late parties could not offend them seriously. Nothing short of a demolition bomb seemed to bother my neighbors.

I lived on room service. But in this, too, there was a disenchantment. Some time between the moment when I ordered dinner over the phone and when it was rolled into my living room like a corpse on a rubber-wheeled table, I lost all interest in it. Once I ordered a sirloin steak and a chocolate sundae, but everything was so cunningly disguised on the table that I mistook the chocolate sauce for gravy and poured it over the sirloin steak.

Of course all this was the more trivial aspect of a spiritual dislocation that began to manifest itself in far more disturbing ways. I soon found myself becoming indifferent to people. A well of cynicism rose in me. Conversations all sounded as if they had been recorded years ago and were being played back on a turntable. Sincerity and kindliness seemed to have gone out of my friends' voices. I suspected them of hypocrisy. I stopped calling them, stopped seeing them. I was impatient of what I took to be inane flattery.

I got so sick of hearing people say, "I loved your play!" that I could not say thank you any more. I choked on the words and turned rudely away from the usually sincere person. I no longer felt any pride in the play itself but began to dislike it, probably because I felt too life-less inside ever to create another. I was walking around dead in my shoes and I knew it but there were no friends I knew or trusted sufficiently, at that time, to take them aside and tell them what was the matter.

This curious condition persisted about three months, till late spring, when I decided to have another eye operation mainly because of the excuse it gave me to withdraw from the world behind a gauze mask. It was my fourth eye operation, and perhaps I should explain that I had been afflicted for about five years with a cataract on my left eye which required a series of needling operations and finally an operation on the muscle of the eye. (The eye is still in my head. So much for that.)

Well, the gauze mask served a purpose. While I was resting in the hospital the friends whom I had neglected or affronted in one way or another began to call on me, and now that I was in pain and darkness, their voices seemed to have changed, or rather that unpleasant mutation which I had suspected earlier in the season had now disappeared and they sounded now as they had used to sound in the lamented days of my obscurity. Once more they were sincere and kindly voices with the ring of truth in them and that quality of understanding for which I had originally sought them out.

As far as my physical vision was concerned, this last operation was only relatively successful (although it left me with an apparently clear black pupil in the right position, or nearly so) but in another, figurative way, it had served a much deeper purpose.

When the gauze mask was removed I found myself in a readjusted world. I checked out of the handsome suite at the first-class hotel, packed my papers and a few incidental belongings, and left for Mexico, an elemental country where you can quickly forget the false dignities and conceits imposed by success, a country where vagrants innocent as children curl up to sleep on the pavements and human voices, especially when their language is not familiar to the ear, are soft as birds'. My public self, that artifice of mirrors, did not exist here and so my natural being was resumed.

Then, as a final act of restoration, I settled for a while at Chapala to work on a play called *The Poker Night,* which later became *A Streetcar Named Desire.* It is only in his work that an artist can find reality and satisfaction, for the actual world is less intense than the world of his invention, and consequently his life, without recourse to violent disorder, does not seem very substantial. The right condition for him is that in which his work is not only convenient but unavoidable.

For me a convenient place to work is a remote place among strangers where there is good swimming. But life should require a certain minimal effort. You should not have too many people waiting on you; you should have to do most things for yourself. Hotel service is embarrassing. Maids, waiters, bellhops, porters, and so forth are the most embarrassing people in the world for they continually remind you of inequities which we accept as the proper thing. The sight of an ancient woman, gasping and wheezing as she drags a heavy pail of water down a hotel corridor to mop up the mess of some drunken overprivileged guest, is one that sickens and weighs upon the heart and withers it with shame for this world in which it is not only tolerated but regarded as proof positive that the wheels of Democracy are functioning as they should without interference from above or below. Nobody should have to clean up anybody else's mess in this world. It is terribly bad for both parties, but probably worse for the one receiving the service.

I have been corrupted as much as anyone else by the vast number of menial services which our society has grown to expect and depend on. We should do for ourselves or let the machines do for us—the glorious technology that is supposed to be the new light of the world. We are like a man who has bought a great amount of equipment for a camping trip, who has the canoe and the tent and the fishing lines and the axe and the guns, the mackinaw and the blankets, but who now, when all the preparations and the provisions are piled expertly together, is suddenly too timid to set out on the journey but remains where he was yesterday and the day before and day before that, looking suspiciously through white lace curtains at the clear sky he distrusts. Our great technology is a God-given chance for adventure and for progress which we are afraid to attempt. Our ideas and our ideals remain exactly what they were and where they were three centuries ago. No. I beg your pardon. It is no longer safe for a man to even declare them!

This is a long excursion from a small theme into a large one which I did not intend to make, so let me go back to what I was saying before.

This is an oversimplification. One does not escape that easily from the seduction of an effete way of life. You cannot arbitrarily say to yourself, I will now continue my life as it was before this thing, Success, happened to me. But once you fully apprehend the vacuity of a life without struggle you are equipped with the basic means of salvation. Once you know this is true, that the heart of man, his body and his brain, are forged in a white-hot furnace for the purpose of conflict (the struggle of creation) and that with the conflict removed, the man is a sword cutting daisies, that not privation but luxury is the wolf at the door and that the fangs of this wolf are all the little vanities and conceits and laxities that Success is heir to—why, then with this knowledge you are at least in a position of knowing where danger lies.

You know, then, that the public Somebody you are when you "have a name" is a fiction created with mirrors and that the only somebody worth being is the solitary and unseen you that existed from your first breath and which is the sum of your actions and so is constantly in a state of becoming under your own volition—and knowing these things, you can even survive the catastrophe of Success!

It is never altogether too late, unless you embrace the Bitch Goddess, as William James called her, with both arms and find in her smothering caresses exactly what the homesick little boy in you always wanted, absolute protection and utter effortlessness. Security is a kind of death, I think, and it can come to you in a storm of royalty checks beside a kidney-shaped pool in Beverly Hills or anywhere at all that is removed from the conditions that made you an artist, if that's what you are or were or intended to be. Ask anyone who has experienced the kind of success I am talking about—What good is it? Perhaps to get an honest answer you will have to give him a shot of truth serum but the word he will finally groan is unprintable in genteel publications.

Then what is good? The obsessive interest in human affairs, plus a certain amount of compassion and moral conviction, that first made the experience of living something that must be translated into pigment or music or bodily movement or poetry or prose or anything that's dynamic and expressive—that's what's good for you if you're at all serious in your aims. William Saroyan wrote a great play on this theme, that purity of heart is the one success worth having. "In the time of your life—live!" That time is short and it doesn't return again. It is slipping away while I write this and while you read it, and the monosyllable of the clock is Loss, loss, loss, unless you devote your heart to its opposition.

1947

HIGH SCHOOL GUIDE

TO

The Glass Menagerie

ABOUT THE HIGH SCHOOL GUIDE

Tennessee Williams writes plays that are meant to be read aloud. While reading the simple prose, it becomes clear that the subtext and underlying complexity belie the initial perception of the plays. Students enjoy grappling with the complex characters who evoke sympathy from the audience on one page and rage on the next. The classroom bubbles with conversation, debate, and emotion when we read and discuss any Tennessee Williams play, one of the many reasons I advocate teaching his work in high schools and colleges.

This high school edition brings together historical context, focus areas, and critical reception. Each scene begins with useful vocabulary to know before reading, and each scene ends with chronological questions for discussion of the play. Corresponding page numbers from the script are indicated in parentheses. Finally, each scene offers questions for additional exploration through writing. After the play, you'll find relevant reviews and essays along with more questions and writing prompts.

In this publication we strive to present to you an easy way to integrate this play into the high school curriculum. These questions and resources exist to promote lively discussions and thoughtful writing responses in the classroom. For many of the prompts, multiple answers exist. We hope this compilation of context, criticism, and questions allows for enhanced enjoyment of this remarkable play.

Happy Reading,
Kate Walker

BEFORE READING

A Discussion of the Introduction by Robert Bray

NOTE TO TEACHERS: There are three ways to use this introduction (beginning on page 1). Students can read this before beginning the play, so they will have an outline of the entire play and a sense of motifs to look for as they read. Paragraphs 1–7 provide useful background information. However, paragraphs 8–13 outline the play and events in it. Therefore, a second way to approach reading this introduction would be to read the first half and hold off on the second half until after you've finished the play to avoid spoilers about the plot. A final option would be to read this introduction in full after a first reading and before rereading the play.

Vocabulary to know: *calamitous* (1); *penury* (1); *hapless* (1); *lobotomy* (1); *legerdemain* (2); *adulation* (2); *bemused* (2); *aesthetic* (2); *emulate* (2); *mise-en-scène* (2); *prosaic* (3); *protean* (3); *propitious* (3); *catharsis* (3); *wrenching* (3); *oeuvre* (4); *analogous* (4); *leitmotif* (4); *fissure* (4); *ameliorate* (5); *exigency* (5); *facile* (6); *banal* (6); *ephemeral* (6); *dalliance* (6).

QUESTIONS FOR DISCUSSION

1. What do we learn about Williams's personal experience that might have impacted the content of the play?
2. Why does Bray propose American audiences were ready for William's voice? (para 4)
3. What does it mean when Bray writes "Tennessee Williams cer-

tainly realized that positioning crises of the heart within the immediate family would provide ample material for audience empathy and catharsis, as virtually anyone can identify with similar levels of emotional content"? Can you think of specific examples of other books, plays, shows, or films that demonstrate a crisis "of the heart within the immediate family"? (para 5)

4. Bray considers Williams's plays "as an organic holograph" (4) and then compares it to works by Monet and Gauguin. Look up those paintings he refers to and then explain what he means by calling the play "embellished from experience." (4)

5. In alluding to the Ancient Mariner's albatross, what does Bray imply in terms of how Tom (and Tennessee) might have viewed his relationship and responsibility to his sister?

6. Why might Tennessee Williams have referred to this play as a "quiet play," as noted by Bray?

Timeline of Tennessee Williams's Life

March 26, 1911: Thomas Lanier Williams III is born to Cornelius Coffin Williams and Edwina Estelle Dakin Williams in Columbus, Mississippi; his sister Rose is two years old.

July 1918: The Williams family moves to St. Louis, Missouri, where his brother, Walter Dakin Williams, is born the next year.

1928: Thomas Lanier Williams's short story, "The Vengeance of Nitocris," is published in *Weird Tales* magazine. And in July Williams's grandfather, Walter Edwin Dakin (1857–1954), takes young Tom on a tour of Europe.

September 1929: Tom begins classes at the University of Missouri at Columbia, but in the summer of 1932 Tom fails ROTC and is taken out of college by his father and put to work as a clerk at the International Shoe Company.

January 1936: He enrolls in extension courses at Washington University, St. Louis.

March 18 and 20, 1937: His first full-length play, *Candles to the Sun*, is produced by the Mummers, a semi-professional theater company in St. Louis. In September, Tom transfers to the University of Iowa and *Fugitive Kind* is performed by the Mummers.

In 1938 Tom graduates from the University of Iowa with an English degree and completes the play *Not About Nightingales*.

1939: *Story* magazine publishes "The Field of Blue Children" with the first printed use of his professional name, "Tennessee Williams." He receives an award from the Group Theatre for a group of short plays,

"American Blues," which leads to his association with Audrey Wood, his agent for the next thirty-two years.

January through June 1940: Tennessee studies playwriting with John Gassner and Erwin Piscator at the New School for Social Research in New York City. And on December 30 *Battle of Angels,* starring Miriam Hopkins, suffers a disastrous first night during its out-of-town tryout in Boston and closes shortly thereafter.

December 1942: At a cocktail party given by Lincoln Kirstein in New York, Tennessee meets James Laughlin, the founder of New Directions Publishing, who becomes Williams's lifelong friend and publisher.

1943: He drafts a screen treatment of his work-in-progress, *The Gentleman Caller,* while under contract in Hollywood with Metro Goldwyn Mayer. Rejected by the studio, he later rewrites it as *The Glass Menagerie.*

December 26, 1944: *The Glass Menagerie* opens in Chicago starring Laurette Taylor and is immediately hailed as a remarkably original success.

March 31, 1945: *The Glass Menagerie* opens on Broadway and goes on to win the Drama Critics Circle Award for best play of the year. In December 27 *Wagons Full of Cotton and Other Plays* is published.

Summer 1947: He meets Frank Merlo (1929–1963) in Provincetown—starting in 1948 they become lovers and companions and remain together for fourteen years.

On December 3, 1947: *A Streetcar Named Desire,* directed by Elia Kazan and starring Jessica Tandy, Marlon Brando, Kim Hunter, and Karl Malden, opens on Broadway to rave reviews and wins the Pulitzer Prize and the Drama Critics Circle Award. Arthur Miller later famously stated, "What *Streetcar*'s first production did was to plant the flag of beauty on the shores of commercial theater."

1950: The novel *The Roman Spring of Mrs. Stone* is published and the film version of *The Glass Menagerie* is released.

February 3, 1951: *The Rose Tattoo* opens on Broadway starring Maureen Stapleton and Eli Wallach and wins the Tony Award for best play of the year. Later that year, the film version of *A Streetcar Named Desire* is released starring Vivian Leigh as Blanche and Marlon Brando as Stanley.

March 24, 1955: *Cat on a Hot Tin Roof* opens on Broadway directed by Elia Kazan and starring Barbara Bel Geddes, Ben Gazzara, and Burl Ives. *Cat* wins the Pulitzer Prize and the Drama Critics Circle Award. The film version of *The Rose Tattoo*, for which Anna Magnani later wins an Academy Award, is released.

1956: The film *Baby Doll*, with a screenplay by Williams and directed by Elia Kazan, is blacklisted by Catholic leader Cardinal Spellman. June: *In the Winter of Cities*, Williams's first book of poetry, is published.

March 10, 1959: *Sweet Bird of Youth* opens on Broadway and runs for three months. The film version of *Suddenly Last Summer*, with a screenplay by Gore Vidal, starring Katharine Hepburn, Elizabeth Taylor, and Montgomery Cliff, is released.

December 29, 1961: *The Night of the Iguana* opens on Broadway and runs for nearly ten months. Earlier that year the film versions of *Summer and Smoke* and *The Roman Spring of Mrs. Stone* are released, followed in 1962 by movies of *Sweet Bird of Youth* and *Period of Adjustment*.

January 15, 1963: *The Milk Train Doesn't Stop Here Anymore* opens on Broadway, starring Tallulah Bankhead, and immediately closes due to a blizzard and a newspaper strike. September: Frank Merlo dies of lung cancer.

March 27, 1968: *Kingdom of Earth* opens on Broadway under the title *The Seven Descents of Myrtle*.

May 11, 1969: *In the Bar of a Tokyo Hotel* opens off-Broadway and runs for three weeks.

September 1969: Tennessee is committed to the Renard Psychiatric Division of Barnes Hospital in St. Louis for three months by his brother Dakin. That same year, Tennessee is awarded a Doctor of Humanities degree by the University of Missouri and the American Academy of Arts and Letters' Gold Medal for Drama.

April 2, 1972: *Small Craft Warnings* opens off-Broadway and runs for a total of six months.

March 1, 1973: *Out Cry*, a revised version of *The Two-Character Play*, opens March 1 on Broadway and runs for just over a week.

June 1975: *The Red Devil Battery Sign* closes during its out-of-town tryout in Boston.

May 11, 1977: *Vieux Carré* opens on Broadway and closes within five days.

1979: Williams is presented with a Lifetime Achievement Award at the Kennedy Center Honors in Washington by President Jimmy Carter.

March 26, 1980: Williams's last Broadway play, *Clothes for a Summer Hotel,* opens and closes after 15 performances.

August 24, 1981: *Something Cloudy, Something Clear* premieres off-Broadway at the Jean Cocteau Repertory Theatre.

May 8, 1982: Williams's last full-length play, *A House Not Meant to Stand*, opens for a limited run at Chicago's Goodman Theatre.

February 25, 1983: Tennessee Williams is found dead in his room at the Hotel Elysée in New York City. It is determined from an autopsy that the playwright died from an overdose of barbiturates. Williams is later buried in St. Louis.

"The Author Tells Why It Is Called The Glass Menagerie" *(1945)*

[From *New Selected Essays: Where I Live* by Tennessee Williams.]

When my family first moved to St. Louis from the South, we were forced to live in a congested apartment neighborhood. It was a shocking change, for my sister and myself were accustomed to spacious yards, porches, and big shade trees. The apartment we lived in was about as cheerful as an Arctic winter. There were outside windows only in the front room and kitchen. The Rooms between had windows that opened upon a narrow areaway that was virtually sunless and which we grimly named "Death Valley" for a reason which is amusing only in retrospect.

There were a great many alley cats in the neighborhood which were constantly fighting the dogs. Every now and then some unwary young cat would allow itself to be pursued into this areaway which had only one opening. The end of the cul-de-sac was directly beneath my sister's bedroom window and it was here that the cats would have to turn around to face their pursuers in mortal combat. My sister would be awakened in the night by the struggle and the in the morning the hideously mangled victim would be lying under her window. Sight of the areaway had become so odious to her, for this reason, that she kept the shade constantly drawn so that the interior of her bedroom had a perpetual twilight atmosphere. Something had to be done to relieve this gloom. So my sister and I painted all her furniture white; she put white curtains at the window and on the shelves around the room she collected a large assortment of little glass articles, of which she was particularly fond. Eventually, the room took on a light and delicate appearance, in spite of the lack of outside illumination, and it became the only room in the house that I found pleasant to enter.

When I left home a number of years later, it was this room that I recalled most vividly and poignantly when looking back on our home life in St. Louis. Particularly the little glass ornaments on the shelves. They were mostly little glass animals. By poetic association they came to represent, in my memory, all the softest emotions that belong to recollection of things past. They stood for all the small and tender things that relieve the austere pattern of life and make it endurable to the sensitive. The areaway where the cats were torn to pieces was one thing—my sister's white curtains and tiny menagerie of glass were another. Somewhere between them was the world that we lived in.

* * *

1. What shocked Tennessee Williams about his move to St. Louis?
2. Why was the alleyway an "odious" place?
3. What did his sister's room in St. Louis represent for Tennessee Williams?
4. How does the juxtaposition of the "mortal combat of alley cats" and the glass menagerie function to explain the title of the play?

Cultural Context for The Glass Menagerie

The *Glass Menagerie* occurs in St. Louis in the 1930s, although Williams wrote it in the mid-1940s, before the conclusion of World War II. (For more information about his own experience, see the essay "The Author Tells Why it is Called *The Glass Menagerie*.") The Great Depression casts a shadow over this play, so understanding what happened during that time period is significant to understanding the cultural context of the play. In 1929, the unregulated and uninsured banks failed and the stock market crashed. Capitalism had failed the people—the working people. Over five thousand banks closed, along with many businesses. Employees were laid off or fired. While not the only reason the Depression began, the stock market crash serves as a marker of what the next ten years would hold: lack of financial security. Between one quarter and one third of Americans were unemployed in 1933. Production fell and people were out of work, hungry, and frustrated.

The lack of jobs impacted living spaces. Tenement housing, or multi-family housing, like the one we see in *Glass Menagerie*, were common in urban areas as they could be built quick and cheap. When people couldn't afford housing, they created shantytowns, called "Hoovervilles," named after President Herbert Hoover, whom many blamed for their dire situation. Hoover exacerbated the economic crisis by attacking people who just wanted what was owed to them. In 1932, veterans of the first World War marched on Washington, demanding payment for government bonus certificates issued during the war (these certificates were not due for years, but people needed money and food immediately). Hoover ordered the army to drive out the marchers (made up of veterans, wives, and children) and the troops released tear gas, set fire to buildings, and shot two veterans. The next election cycle saw to it that Hoover would not return to office after his inability to help the economy.

When President Franklin Delano Roosevelt took office in 1933, the economic situation was bleak, but his New Deal program, designed to reform the country, helped reorganize industry and provide jobs. (And during his tenure, when a small group of veterans marched on Washington, Roosevelt had coffee with them and sent them on their way, without violence.) The Public Works Administration, among many other laws and agencies, helped put people back to work. He created a National Recovery Act to help the economy (although after two years, the Supreme Court ruled it unconstitutional). These actions stabilized the economy and helped the lower classes, who were on the verge of rebellion against the government. While many of Roosevelt's actions helped big business, workers did see some improvements, but not enough to stop major strikes from happening all over the country. This is why, in 1935, The Wagner Act was introduced to set up the National Labor Relations Board, which would help stabilize the labor disruptions due to strikes. Along with unions, this helped workers gain rights and helped companies maintain order. The Social Security Act of 1935 also established some safeguards for employees, such as unemployment insurance and care for the disabled.

During this decade, St. Louis suffered in the same way as the rest of the country. Steel mills laid off workers, many of whom were black. In the early 1930s, unemployment in St. Louis was almost ten percent higher than the national average, and many black workers were denied jobs based on racial discrimination. In St. Louis, marches were held, homeless shelters were overflowing, and when jobs became available, hundreds applied for them. A Hooverville of almost 5000 people sprung up along the Mississippi River. Crisis relief centers handed out food to hungry people, but the city could hardly keep up with the needs of the poor.

Aside from the economic issues, a drought was ravaging the farms of America. John Steinbeck wrote about this in his novel *The Grapes of Wrath* where he chronicled the impact of the Dust Bowl as people abandoned their farms, moved in droves out west to California, and looked for work.

In the decade before the second World War, many people's daily lives seemed bleak and so they turned to entertainment as an escape. In St. Louis, churches held variety shows just to give the homeless something to do with their time. Radio shows were free (if you had a radio) and many people spent time listening to popular stories like Amos 'N Andy and Little Orphan Annie. If people could afford it, they might go to the movies. Theatres ran double features, and even triple features, and they also offered door prizes for theatre-goers. Considering movies only cost a quarter, the appeal of hours of entertainment and possible prizes drew large crowds to movie theatres. Some of the most famous actors and actresses of this decade include Shirley Temple, Charlie Chaplin, Ginger Rogers, Fred Astaire, Bette Davis, Errol Flynn, Mae West, Jean Harlow, Clark Gable, Marlene Dietrich, and Gary Cooper. Listed below are some movies from this decade:

1930—*The Big Trail, Hell's Angels, Danger Lights*
1931—*Frankenstein, Dracula, The Public Enemy, Mata Hari*
1932—*The Mummy, Scarface, Tarzan, Grand Hotel, The Most Dangerous Game*
1933—*King Kong, Flying Down to Rio, The Invisible Man, Duck Soup*
1934—*It Happened One Night, The Thin Man, The Man Who Knew Too Much*
1935—*The 39 Steps, Mutiny on the Bounty, A Night at the Opera*
1936—*Swing Time, Flash Gordon, Reefer Madness, Mr. Deeds Goes to Town*
1937—*Snow White and the Seven Dwarfs, Heidi, Shall We Dance*
1938—*The Adventures of Robin Hood, You Can't Take it With You, Holiday*
1939—*Gone with the Wind, The Wizard of Oz, Mr. Smith Goes to Washington*

Many of these films offered plots with escapism and comedy, allowing the viewers to imagine themselves in a different world for a few hours.

Circumstances changed as the 1930s ended and industries geared up for war—more jobs became available. In 1939, Germany attacked Poland, but the United States did not enter the war until the Japanese bombed Pearl Harbor, Hawaii, on December 7, 1941. They joined the other Allied countries in the war against the Axis powers. By joining the war, the United States ushered in a war-time economy, which helped stabilize the improving economy. While the New Deal reduced unemployment (from 13 million to 9 million) it was the war that really boosted the economy and helped the workers. In St. Louis, unemployment fell to less than four percent, a more than 30% drop.

As you read *The Glass Menagerie*, keep in mind what the characters might have experienced in their daily lives based on cultural context. The world they lived in differs from our current world. Understanding those differences can help us understand why they might have acted and reacted in ways different from how we might act and react today.

QUESTIONS FOR FURTHER EXPLORATION

1. If unemployment rates were high, how easy or difficult would it have been to get a job in St. Louis in this era?
2. Look up details about the New Deal and consider how those new policies might have impacted the lives of the characters in this play.
3. Find out the plot to one of the movies listed above and write a paragraph about how viewers might see it as an escape from their present reality.

WORKS CONSULTED

"Most Popular Feature Films Released 1930–1939." *IMDB.*
Zinn, Howard. *People's History of the United States.* Harper Collins, 2005.

Pre-Reading Activities

UNDERSTANDING THE EPIGRAPH

An epigraph (page 9) appears at the beginning of a book, a play, or a chapter and usually hints at the theme. Below is the full text of the poem by E. E. Cummings from which Williams takes his epigraph.

somewhere i have never travelled,gladly beyond
E. E. Cummings

somewhere i have never travelled,gladly beyond
any experience,your eyes have their silence:
in your most frail gesture are things which enclose me,
or which i cannot touch because they are too near

your slightest look easily will unclose me
though i have closed myself as fingers,
you open always petal by petal myself as Spring opens
(touching skilfully,mysteriously)her first rose

or if your wish be to close me, i and
my life will shut very beautifully, suddenly,
as when the heart of this flower imagines
the snow carefully everywhere descending;

nothing which we are to perceive in this world equals
the power of your intense fragility:whose texture
compels me with the colour of its countries,
rendering death and forever with each breathing

(i do not know what it is about you that closes
and opens;only something in me understands
the voice of your eyes is deeper than all roses)
nobody,not even the rain,has such small hands

1. Describe the person the speaker addresses in this poem using specific lines.
2. What is the relationship between the speaker and the subject of this poem? Use specific lines to support your claim.
3. Consider the significance of the last line of the poem. What kind of theme does that hint at for the play?

UNPACKING THE CHARACTER DESCRIPTIONS (page 11)

1. For each character, list the adjectives used to describe them. Look for examples of these qualities as you read the play.
2. Why might there be more description for the two women in the play?
3. What predictions do you have about the play, based on these character descriptions?

UNPACKING THE PRODUCTION NOTES (page 13)

1. Williams describes this as a memory play—what do you think that means about the content?
2. Why does Williams believe the screen device has value in the production of the play?
3. How does Williams want the music to function? Do you think it is possible for music to express the emotion and nostalgia he wants it to express?
4. What is significant about the type of light Williams wants projected on Laura's character? How might this impact the audience's perception of her?

READING THE PLAY

BEFORE EACH SCENE
Images from the Play, Vocabulary to Know

AFTER EACH SCENE
Discussion Questions While Reading,
Writing Prompts

SCENE 1 (page 17)

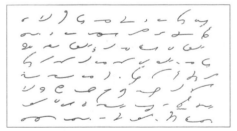

Gregg shorthand diagram

Merchant marine

Vocabulary to know: *conglomeration* (17); *implacable* (17); *proscenium* (17); *portieres* (17); *matriculate* (18); *masticate* (20); *nimble* (21); *elegiac* (22); *beaux* (22); *old maid* (23).

SCENE 1 — DISCUSSION QUESTIONS

1. In the initial stage directions:
   a. What commentary does Williams make about the Wingfield family's apartment?
   b. What comparisons does he draw with the metaphors he uses?
   c. What is the overall tone of these stage directions? Refer to specific words.
2. In Tom's opening monologue:
   a. Why might he call himself the opposite of a stage magician? How does that set the tone for the audience?
   b. What does he think about the middle class in the 1930s?
   c. What do you think about the words on the postcard from Tom's father?
   d. Why would Tennessee Williams use Tom to introduce us to the play and the concept of a memory play?
3. What might be the significance of the stage direction for the "legend on screen" *où sont les neiges,* which, according to the Merriam Webster dictionary, translates to: *where are last year's snows? where has the past gone?*
4. Characterize Amanda:
   a. How does she treat her children? Does she treat her son and daughter differently? Why call Laura sister instead of daughter?
   b. What does it mean when Amanda's voice becomes elegiac? What is she mourning?
   c. Why might Amanda insist some kind of flood or tornado keeps gentleman callers away?
5. Laura doesn't say much in this scene, but in the stage directions, Williams writes *"Laura nervously echoed her laugh. She slips in a fugitive manner through the half-open portieres."* What does this stage direction tell us about her character and her relationship with her mother?
6. Describe Tom and Laura's relationship based on their interactions in this scene.

SCENE 1 — WRITING PROMPTS

1. Do you identify with any of the characters in the play? Why or why not?

2. Does this first scene and/or the characters remind you of any other text you've read or watched? Do any characters seem to match archetypal characters?

3. How do the topics of conversation in this scene compare to modern day conversations?

4. In the production notes, Williams describes *The Glass Menagerie* music as "the most delicate music in the world and the saddest." He explains it should evoke the understanding in the audience of: "how beautiful it is and how easily it can be broken." With this in mind, what song might you use for this if you were the director, as it closes out this first scene? Explain.

SCENE 2 (page 24)

Cloche hat   Victrola

Vocabulary to know: *grim* (24); *D.A.R.* (24); *martyr* (24); *induct* (26); *humility* (28); *grudging* (28); *pleurosis* (29); *vivacity* (29).

SCENE 2 — DISCUSSION QUESTIONS

1. Why does the stage direction include Laura polishing her glass and then hiding that and pretending to type when Amanda arrives?
2. What does it tell us about Amanda when Williams includes "a bit of acting" when describing Amanda when she arrives home (24)?
3. Why might Laura attempt to put music on when her mother chastises her?
4. What could the D.A.R. represent for Amanda?
5. Do you think Laura's limp keeps her from living a full life?

SCENE 2 — WRITING PROMPTS

1. Unpack Amanda's speech about the "Crust of Humility" on 28 and 29. What is the purpose of her tirade?
2. Have you ever dropped out of something and not wanted to tell your parents? Why would Laura refrain from telling her mother she dropped out of typing school?
3. In Amanda's speech, she worries about "dependency." In what ways do we see both dependence and independence from Laura?
4. Should Laura have dropped out? Do you think she should return to the class?
5. There are inflation calculators online to show how much $50 is worth today (about $850 in 2017). Does that impact your opinion of Laura's actions?

SCENE 3 (page 30)

Etruscan sculpture

Vocabulary to know: *fiasco* (30); *archetype* (30); *specter* (30); *turgid* (32); *precipitate* (32); *gesticulate* (32); *insolence* (33); *celotex* (33); *pinion* (34).

SCENE 3 — DISCUSSION QUESTIONS

1. What is significant about Amanda selling women's magazines, considering what those magazines contain?
2. Is Amanda a good salesperson? Why or why not?
3. Amanda takes away a D. H. Lawrence novel from Tom. This could well be *Lady Chatterley's Lover*. If that was the book, why might the theme be significant for Tom?
4. What sacrifices does Tom make for his family?
5. What might the movies represent for Tom?
6. How does Amanda act when Tom argues with her? How does she treat him? Is this a typical mother-son relationship?

SCENE 3 — WRITING PROMPTS

1. This scene contains a power struggle between Tom and Amanda. What are the complexities of their power dynamic?
2. Unpack Tom's hyperbolic speech in this scene. What does this tirade show us about Tom in terms of who he is and what he desires?
3. What might Tom's accidental breaking of some of Laura's glass collection symbolize? What about his reaction to it?
4. At this point in the play, are there characters or situations you have seen in your own life or in other books? What themes about human nature do you see in the play so far?

SCENE 4 (page 36)

A print by Daumier

Vocabulary to know: *motley* (36); *listless* (39); *grotesque* (39); *bower* (40); *brood* (41); *spartan* (41); *querulous* (42); *provisions* (43); *importunate* (44).

SCENE 4 — DISCUSSION QUESTIONS

1. How much of Tom's story of his night do you believe? Does it matter if we believe him?
2. Tom asks: "Who in hell ever got himself out of [a coffin] without removing one nail?" and then the stage direction calls for a light on the father's photo. What does this imply the viewer/reader should think?
3. When Laura slips on the fire escape, what is the difference between how Tom reacts and how Amanda reacts? What does that tell you about them?

4. What does the stage direction for Tom and Amanda's body language show us?
5. What is the one thing Amanda wants Tom's help with before he leaves them?
6. Is Tom selfish, like Amanda says?

SCENE 4 — WRITING PROMPTS

1. How does Amanda demonstrate what we might consider typical mom behavior in this scene?
2. Why do you think Tom craves adventure so much? Do you think this desire for adventure is just part of human nature?
3. Do you agree or disagree with Amanda that "instinct is something that people have to get away from"? (42)
4. Why close the scene with Amanda selling more magazine subscriptions? What might this demonstrate?

SCENE 5 (page 46)

Vocabulary to know: *annunciation* (46); *imminent* (47); *bombardment* (47); *sphinx* (48); *chintz* (50); *supercilious* (52); *discreet* (52); *homely* (53); *ulterior* (54).

SCENE 5 — DISCUSSION QUESTIONS

1. Subtext means someone is implying something they do not explicitly state. What is the subtext of Tom's speech to the audience?
2. Why doesn't Tom tell his mother immediately about the gentleman caller?
3. What does Amanda think is worse than being an old maid? (54) Why?
4. What assumptions does Amanda make about James because he is Irish? Does this type of stereotyping still happen?

SCENE 5 — WRITING PROMPTS

1. How do wishes function in this scene?
2. The idea of the future is raised several times in this scene—what does it represent to different people?
3. Do Tom and Amanda have a typical mother-son relationship?
4. What might the fire escape symbolize?

SCENE 6 (page 56)

Jonquils

Vocabulary to know: *unobtrusive* (56); *devout* (57); *translucent* (57); *solemn* (58); *voile* (58); *cotillion* (59); *sashay* (59); *giddy* (59); *quinine* (59); *ominous* (60); *preposterous* (62); *poise* (64).

SCENE 6 — DISCUSSION QUESTIONS

1. What do we learn that Tom does in secret at work? Does that deepen or change your understanding of his character?
2. Why does Amanda try to stuff Laura's bra?
3. Why does Jim think Tom should take a public speaking class? Does he make a good argument?
4. Why does an image of the Jolly Roger appear on the screen when it does? What does it represent?
5. Based on context clues, what does "gassing" mean? (65)

6. How does Amanda act towards Jim? Support this with specific evidence from the play.
7. Where do we see pathetic fallacy in this scene and what might it indicate?

SCENE 6 — WRITING PROMPTS

1. What does the line "all pretty girls are a trap, a pretty trap, and men expect them to be" reveal about the societal expectations of the time? Have these expectations changed?
2. How would you describe Amanda's tone as she recalls her youth?
3. What do you think Tom means when he says, "people go to the *movies* instead of *moving*"? (65)

SCENE 7 (page 70)

Dance card

Mazda lamp bulbs

Vocabulary to know: *luminous* (70); *negligence* (71); *rhapsodic* (72); *coax* (72); *limelight* (74); *reverent* (78); *beleaguer* (79); *indolent* (81); *eclipse* (83); *abashed* (87); *tumultuous* (88); *stumblejohn* (88); *gingerly* (89); *decorous* (89); *perturbation* (89); *enrapt* (89); *abate* (90).

SCENE 7 — DISCUSSION QUESTIONS

1. When the lights go out, what might that symbolize?
2. What is the difference between being disappointed and being discouraged?
3. Jim seems to think Laura has an inferiority complex. Do you agree? Why or why not?
4. What does Williams mean with the stage direction "Laura struggles visibly with her storm"? What would you tell the actress if you were the director?

5. What is significant about the unicorn losing its horn?
6. After Tom leaves his family, who does he continue to think about wherever he is? Why?

SCENE 7 — WRITING PROMPTS

1. Laura is self-conscious about her leg, but Jim says he never noticed. Do you think this is common, self-consciousness over something other people might not even notice?
2. Do you agree with Jim that "everybody excels in some one thing"? (82)
3. How could what Amanda says, "you live in a dream; you manufacture illusions," be true for each of the characters in this play? (94)
4. When Amanda talks to Laura at the end of the play while Tom gives his speech, what do you think Amanda might be saying to her? Write a few lines of dialogue that she might say quietly to her daughter.

AFTER READING

End of the Play Discussion Questions and Writing Prompts

1. Tennessee Williams uses detailed stage directions to dictate setting, lighting, music, and character reactions. In a recent Broadway production, the director chose to ignore many of those directions, and audience reaction was mixed. Use your search engine to find some recent online reviews as you respond to the question of whether a modern director should adhere to the original stage directions or take liberties with them.

2. Now that you've read the entire play, reconsider the poem by E. E. Cummings "somewhere i have never travelled,gladly beyond" (see page 119 for the poem). Write an analysis explaining why Williams chose the last line of this poem as the epigraph for the play.

3. Throughout the play, legends are projected on to the screen and the stage directions tell the director what should be projected. How do these projections function for the audience? Choose a few specific examples and explain.

4. Williams alludes to a number of paintings and poems in the stage directions. Why might he use other pieces of art to describe the effects he wants to achieve? How might art more efficiently project the mood he wants to achieve rather than just a description?

5. In the introduction, Robert Bray posits: "every character seeks flight; if not literally, then through the imagination" (4). Explore the motif of escape permeating the play. Use specific examples for each character.

6. In the introduction, Bray writes, "Audiences and readers may choose to either demonize Amanda or regard her as a misguided saint" (6). Consider ways in which she might function as both a demon and a saint, and then conclude with your own analysis of her complex character.

7. After carefully considering each character, make an argument for who you might cast in a television or film adaptation today. Why would the actors you choose be suitable for the role you cast them in? Refer to characterization in the play as well as to previous work by each actor.

Critical Reviews/Commentary

1. Use your search engine to find original reviews from 1944 and 1945 in such newspapers as the *Chicago Tribune* and the *New York Times*.

   Consider the metaphors reviewers employed when first encountering *The Glass Menagerie:* choose one metaphor and explain how the reviewer used it to enhance a description of the play's experience.

   Does any review claim *The Glass Menagerie* is a work of art?

   Does any reviewer find flaws in the play? If so, how do the flaws measure up vis-à-vis the overall *Glass Menagerie* experience?

2. Now, research recent performances of *The Glass Menagerie*— revived on Broadway on the spring of 2017—and their reviews.

   Again, do the reviewers find the performance they saw as a work of art? Or as a flawed production? Do they compare this production to previous ones? If so, what are the reviewer's conclusions?